At the Court of the Crow

Dedication

For Aline Lonneville. Kitten.
With all love
Always.
x

JK

At the Court of the Crow

Tanith Lee

IMMANION
PRESS
Stafford England

At the Court of the Crow
By Tanith Lee
© 2020

Cover art by John Kaiine
Cover Design: Danielle Lainton
Interior illustrations by John Kaiine & Danielle Lainton
Interior layout by Storm Constantine

Set in Palatino Linotype

ISBN 978-1-912815-14-2

Catalogue Number: IP0165

An Immanion Press Edition
http://www.immanion–press.com
info@immanion–press.com

Contents

Author's Note

The ambience of this book is a kind of steampunk parallel historical, set about 1915/18, and post some type of, initially, unspecified apocalypse. And certain of its sources derive, of course – given the basic material of fallen angels/demons – from classical texts, a few of which will be apparent even in the first section.

Tanith Lee

Publisher's Note

Some decades ago, Tanith Lee was asked to write a novel with a steampunk ambience, and this book is the result of her writing the first three chapters. After that, she realised her heart wasn't in this story. She yearned to write something else. So, *At the Court of the Crow* languished for years in Tanith's records. She never found the inspiration to continue with it.

However, the chapters she did write form a neat novella, and for this reason her husband, John Kaiine, asked Immanion Press to publish it. It's something Tanith fans will love and deserves to see the light of day, if only because we won't be getting any new stories from Tanith now.

Immanion Press is proud to present this strange and wonderous little story. May you all enjoy it.

Storm Constantine, Editor, 2020

The Marble Garden

1

The Marble Garden

During the night I was often woken by the thud and smash of stars falling on the roof.

My room was the highest in the house, up among the attics. The others were seldom disturbed.

That morning I got up early, about 2 am, and gazed from the window. The sky was not yet thinking about lightening, but the raw flames of the still-fastened stars burned metallic pink and copper. The moon was down, and the Planet balefully floated above my Uncle's barn.

Pieces of the fallen stars lay like broken glass along the porch steps, and over the grey lawn.

I saw at once too the frere pig had got loose again.

It was scuttling along under the wall of the fruit-garden, shaking the bushes there. It saw me looking and cast me one of its devilish glances. We were not friends, the frere pig and I, but then it liked no one. Lifting its hind trotter at the gate post, it let go a stream of steaming silver piddle – its insides must be molten – then rushed through the break in the gate. The pig would have the skin off the winter apple, as it had last time. But then, Cob should have mended the gate. It was hardly my fault. I should pretend I had not seen.

But what to do until sunrise? I lay back down on my hard bed and stared up at the shadowy ceiling.

When I was little, and had first been brought to Uncle Euthon's house on the back of Blutch's donkey, I had been afraid of the place at once. It was a horrible filthy old house too, flat-faced and pale, with craning black chimney stacks, and rows of windows like a pack of blank glass cards. Cobwebs hung inside and out. No sooner was I in, a terrified child of six, than a huge whyvit's nest had plunged down the hall chimney and landed on the hearth. When I screamed, Aunt Caris had shouted through the smoke and flinders at me, to be quiet and 'contain myself'. But Plooty, who was only nine years older than I, murmured I was a poor soul and had already seen horrors, Mistress Caris should be kinder. Plooty then took me to the kitchens, and in the red light of an unspoilt fire, took off my damp cloak and shoes, and gave me applenog and a biscuit. But I was afraid of Plooty then, too, with her dry face and pointed nose and hair like black rope. I was afraid of all of it, and everything.

And to be honest, (since I had better be, now) aged twenty, fourteen years on from my arrival, on that grey morning as the pig frisked, I was yet afraid of it all, all that house of Euthon's. Of its chimneys and livestock, and of the family also, though they were, I had been well told, my closest kin. So one learns even boredom and distaste do not cast out fear.

"Master Euthon, Cob is at the window," said Plooty, setting down the prail in china bowls.

"So I see. What does the idiot want?"

We had all those of us that was who were alive, turned our eyes to the long yard window-door. There Cob lurked, his large hands dangling from his sleeves and his face a mask of enmity.

"Well, Master Euthon. Shall I let the poor soul in to tell you?"

Uncle Euthon swore by the gravemounds on the hill.

But Plooty undid the glass.

Cob came in, ungainly as a bird-scare, and balanced lopsided on the carpet, reeking of onions and unwashing.

"Well?"

"It's the frere pig, Master. It's in the garden again"

Aunt Caris let out a malevolent shriek.

Euthon spoke. "Then get it out, you fool – go – go on! Or do I take you into the town for another whipping?"

"The difficulty is, Master, its blood is up. It'll have my arm off."

"So shall I, if you don't go and see to it."

"Shall I take a drop of nog to placate the creature?"

Uncle Euthon strode to the cabinet and pulled out an old yellow bottle. "Don't think I don't know who this will go to placate, Cob," he roared, and flung the bottle over our heads.

Cob caught it with no trouble and slouched out again into the cold-stung morning. He disappeared very slowly around one side of the house. We sat listening, and presently heard terrible squeals, shouts and rumbling from the garden, over the yard wall. Plooty closed the glass door and hurried to her kitchens, muttering that an unwatched pot always boils.

"He shall go for a whipping," said Euthon.

"Indeed he should," agreed Caris. "He'll be the better for it."

The breakfast room was long and narrow, filled almost entirely by a long, narrow table, and lemon wall coverings. There were six places laid there, my Uncle and Aunt at head and foot, with between them, to my Uncle's left and my Aunt's right hand, the three chairs of their offspring. My Cousin Wild sat nearest to his father, and my Cousiness Thalvia to her mother. In the middle stood the chair of my other Cousiness Mhayr. But Mhayr was represented by her portrait, painted in her twentieth year, and now carried in always for breakfast by Blutch, and positioned in the chair instead. Mhayr herself had been dead for some time. In the flesh I had never known her.

They were a good-looking family, Wild a long-haired tawny sixteen, Thalvia nineteen, dark-haired and high-coloured, Mhayr a nice, dead blonde. Even Euthon and Caris were not bad-looking, but the decades of pettiness, self-indulgence and self-deception, and evident insanity had not, visually at least, been kind to them.

My chair was on the other long side of the table, directly in the middle, in a sort of island of genetic and spatial loneliness.

I took another spoonful of prail, but it was too salty for me as usual. Caris had given up chiding me for the waste of food; she merely glared.

On the mantlepiece, among the dried curse-flowers and antique vases, the white crescent clock struck for 4 am.

Outside, the daylight stayed wan. A solitary indigo cloud loomed in the sky, full of ill-omen and scratch-hail. In the fruit-garden the awful uproar had not abated.

"Be damned to the fool, what is he doing with that pig?" ranted my Uncle.

"Dancing perhaps," said Thalvia idly.

As if by magic the external pandemonium abruptly ceased.

The frere pig was so often a cause of discord and extreme anxiety. It was kept at my Uncle's expense and chained up (when it might be caught) outside at night, to entice any marauding ratines that would otherwise attack the chicken sheds. The ratines were as large as wolves in those parts, and dangerous, for their bite, which anyway might take off a man's head let alone his arm, was venomous. However, being sometimes sexually partial to frere pigs they would occasionally mate with them, and the resultant hybrids were non-poisonous. They had black barbed fur like that of a pig, a piggish deviousness, a rattish strength, and the violent temperament of both. Such ghastly things were highly prized as guard animals, or for their speed at the races in Flast.

Uncle Euthon drained his blue-tea and rose.

"I shall be in my study."

My Aunt also got up. "Hurry and make yourself ready, Thalvia. If we're to get to town and back before dusk, we must make haste. Good morning, Mhayr." So saying she left the room and Thalvia elegantly trailed after her. Mhayr had to remain where she was, of course.

Wild glanced at me with a mean, acorn-coloured eye. "And you, you slut, what are you planning to do with your day?

I ignored him. The times were gone when, he a child and I fourteen or fifteen, he had pinched and scored me with his nails, spied on me and told lies of me, and tried to frighten me in the dark of the nights by producing ghostly wailings outside my bedroom door. He had other business now, mostly at the neighbouring house only an hour off along the Plain Road. There, three fat daughters liked to entertain him, and their fat brothers to gamble with him until Wild had not a coin left in his pocket. Despite that, Wild still kept a vague vicious interest in me. I was the stranger in the nest after all. I was the unusual girl who did not scaredly try to pacify, or enamouredly try to flatter him: a mystery to be solved.

"I said, you, what'll you be at today?"

I raised my eyes and looked straight into his and straight through them and out the other side.

"Bitch," said he, not liking this. "I'll tell you what. They say at the neighbours' a beastman has been seen. Worse than any ratine, yes? Got hold of a young woman near the town, just a few days back, and ate her nose and fingers. You think of that, Orphan, and do mind how you go outside."

Orphan. That was their name, or Wild and Thalvia's name for me. I forgot to say.

The city of Mephaizium was squadrons of miles and thousands of days' journey to the north. Nearer by very little, and more southerly, lay the city of Shevain. Although I had been hearing of both metropolises since six years of age, I had naturally never gone to either. I only knew the town of Flast, and that not well.

Aunt Caris and Thalvia, (and Mhayr too, presumably, when she lived) went quite often to the town. Here they bought things, and were driven back in the evening, as to in the morning, by Blutch and the donkey carriage. But it was a tedious drive. Each way it cost an hour and a half, and I could already hear Aunt Caris chivvying Thalvia on the stairs with her perpetual truism: "Come along, there are only a hundred minutes in an hour – only a hundred seconds in each minute - I can't make them longer."

I glanced from a window of the hall gallery and saw the pair exit the premises not long after four. But it was Winterspring, and dark fell soon after 2 pm. At no time was the landscape entirely safe, and after sunfall far less so.

One glimpse of the carriage could educate anyone on this score.

The hobsteel roof was curved, to allow sky debris to slide off on any side. The windows were of the same thickened glass as those set in any comfortable home, and also caged by bars. The bodywork was reinforced in various ungainly ways. As for the donkeys, they had been bred for thick, proofed hide, and wore besides body armour and headpieces to which, by then, they were utterly resigned. For some reason, as I watched the carriage, and newly-armoured Blutch checking the cab seat, himself already strapped with his rifler, long-knife, and other accessories for an outing, I recalled my first sight merely of a donkey. It had been that day I was brought to the house. How appalled and horrified I had been, and somehow still was staring at the ensemble now.

But Aunt Caris and my Cousiness positively scampered from the porch, springing over the star wreckage Cob had not yet bothered to sweep away. The two women were dressed in their most glamorous out gowns, cloaks and jewellery. Thalvia's had a crimson theme. My Aunt's was blue and white.

I possessed no fine clothes, only one decent dress – for burials and other ceremonies; no jewellery at all. What did I want with such stuff?

Turning back from the window as Blutch gained the cab seat and the carriage started off, I beheld myself in the heirloom mirror that stood at the gallery's end. A twenty-year-old young woman stood there, neither tall nor short, with long hair bound up on her head. She had two eyes, eyebrows, a nose, (unlike the one Wild's beastman had sampled) lips, a chin... She had a neck, and shawled breasts and a body, two arms and hands, two legs and feet hidden in her skirt. She was of no more interest to me than to anyone else. That was, irrelevant. That was, virtually accidental, a mistake.

In the conservatory, the dead, dried lacquered plants stood tall and proud, painted in beautiful colours, or glossy black. An occasional stone nymph or goblin sheltered unsuccessfully between their petrified leaves.

On an ironwork table, teacups had been left for days, with dregs in them of blue-tea. Plooty, in her own way, was as careless and indolent as Cob. Only Blutch served the family with any semblance of duty. But he had been one of the Prince's Guard of Life. An old injury had invalided him from the service, and Uncle Euthon, then a well-off scholar who often visited Flast, snapped Blutch up as a bodyguard and general protector. This had happened before ever I washed up in the house.

Depressed for some reason by the dirty sticky cups, and as usual overawed by the mummified foliage, I undid the strengthened glass door and stepped outside.

It was now approaching 5 am, and the sun was high, reaching for the zenith of midday at 6.

It was a white morning of stinging ice. The indigo cloud had enveloped all the east – it seemed in pursuit of the sun, but as yet no hail had come down.

Just beyond the terrace I trod on a bit of star.

It crunched unnervingly underfoot and spat off a tiny spray of sparks.

I went curiously to the fruit-garden, opening the broken gate and wandering along the paths among the orchard of winter apple, quince and tomato trees. There were blossoms on the lower boughs, but not the upper; it would be too exposed and icy there. Some greenish little fruits were ripening, but less, I thought, than in previous Wintersprings. The frere pig too had again caused a lot of damage, goring the trunk and over-skin of the winter apple, and tearing down a whole lemon vine from the wall. Its spiteful little shed bristles lined the herb beds, like splinters of iron.

Wild had asked me what I should do with my day. But what did I ever do? I went about the near places of the house or simply sat in the library, where the fire would only be lit if I did it myself. The books were quite old. The majority had fallen to pieces. One took down a fat cover from a shelf and found inside only fragments, if sometimes very intriguing ones, for example: *'He sprang from the train, and as his knees collided with the ground, a vast abyss,'* After which nothing, nor any clue as to whether a corresponding fragment still remained and might be found. Even should it exist, finding it must be a hopeless dream.

I strayed on over the grounds and passed the chicken sheds. Several days of each week the fowl were let out in special rooms of the house, the Chicken Hall. Here they received fresher air from opened vanes in the roof. But it would hardly be sensible to release them out here, or even into the yard Things were always prowling the Plain that might get in; stikers or plumes, stink-frogs and snakes. Then there was the nocturnal chance of ratines, wolves or quorels.

I reconsidered Wild's threat of the rumoured beastman. These were said, (by my Uncle), to be inventions. No such being could survive. I too, though I seldom agreed with any utterance of Euthon's, believed them unlikely. Yet, when I turned from the iron and steel of the chicken sheds, abruptly my spine began to prickle, as if one of the barbs of the pig had dropped inside my dress.

Only after a moment or so did I allow myself to look behind me.

There was nothing there. Merely the low inner boundary of the sheds. Beyond, outside the grove of violet trees, the other tall and plated wall began, that marked the edges of the grounds. Outside this I could see the higher slopes of the chalky Plain, and about a quarter mile off the gash of the Plain Road, which lead away all that exhausting hour and a half between the hills to Flast.

There was a paunchy wind blowing. Little filmy eddies of chalk and dust furred off the Plain and sailed briefly, simply to fall again to the earth.

I could also note one very big star, or else a big

group of stars, that had crashed on Pitch Hill where the road veered eastward.

The dark blue cloud had almost reached the sun as it struggled towards midday. Soon scratch-hail would strafe the area.

Over in his luxurious barn I could hear the frere pig grooming himself smugly.

And again – my spine spangled.

But I would not turn this time.

Instead I walked swiftly back towards the house and let myself in at the east door.

I lunched on bread and dripping and a cup of tea, which I took from the front kitchen. Plooty was there, emptying the teapot on the back kitchen floor, while whistling a popular song. Her one-eyed ratcat sat on the table licking out a bowl.

"Has Cob checked the boundary wall?" I asked.

Nothing out of the ordinary in that. Caris or Euthon were always demanding to be told.

Had he checked it this month was more the question. Cob was lazy and feckless, less a useful person than an essential eyesore that somehow reassured by its presence. But all the house-people were clannish, even Blutch. You could say nothing against one to any other of them or they would sulk. In my case, Plooty would have flared up angrily, and have me 'know how hard Cob, poor soul, worked his hands to the bone in the service of the family'.

"I think I saw a stiker by the outhouses," I ventured.

"Oh, I doubt you did Girlums." (*Girlums* was *her* childhood name for me, coined when Plooty was only fifteen. "No, when there's nothing in, I'd have seen, wouldn't I, When I fed those chickens? They make a proper old fuss if anything's about, and today they're nearly quiet as silence."

In the library, I did not light the fire. My Aunt had taken to upbraiding me for the waste of coal: if I was chilled could I not sit in the hall where a fire always burned?

The library, fireless, was a big gloomy hollow of a room, lined and divided by high wooden stacks filled with books, or rather those gatherings of fragments I have mentioned. But the windows looked out to three sides of the house, and I went from casement to casement, peering down, trying to see if anything was out there. Nothing was.

Not Cob, of course, he would be at his midday dinner by now.

Uncle Euthon was in his study, reading and writing, and would not emerge until the hour of afternoon tea at sunset.

Wild was long gone along the road on his own donkey, with pistol and whip to hand, making for the jolly neighbours. Probably with luck, we would not see him until tomorrow.

No untoward noises rose from the grounds. Lawn, fruit garden, yard, sheds and barn, the outhouses, the conservatory – all mostly visible from here – showed nothing. But the light was deepening to a rich dense blue as the cloud finally annexed the sun. The violet of the grove of trees seemed to have bled purple up into it too, and now to be dissolving there. The sun itself was only a small bright hole.

Even as I watched, a swathe of hail flailed the landscape. Where it struck the stone of the buildings or yard, or the distant road, little yellowish sizzles of hail fire erupted, dying instantly, then reigniting, in a constant, volatile yet pointless cycle.

A trio of whyvits beat their way desperately across the sky, calling in witch-like voices.

Then I sat down by the cold hearth, curled my cold feet under me, and fell asleep.

I dreamed of a red place, and someone who was shouting but I must not speak or answer. In the dream I thought I was some other person, but who that was I had no idea.

When I woke again, the storm had passed but the windows were darkening now with dusk. The sun was already down.

My Aunt and Cousiness must be home, and I was

surprised not to have been woken before by the clatter and chatter of their return.

Going out, I found the lamps on the upper floor had not been lit.

I could hear some form of activity below. It sounded like Plooty talking and moving quickly to and fro – the swish of her skirt and scuff-scuff of her feet in their battered house-slippers. But also, I thought I heard the low and unmelodic tones of Cob. As usual he seemed full of complaint. Yet it was odd not to pick up my Aunt's shrill voice, or Thalvia's velvety one. Where were they?

Then a door opened directly beneath, on the second floor. It was that of my Uncle's study, and instantly he came out.

I saw him from above, from where I stood in the darkened passage at the stair head. He was completely unaware of me. I had never venerated him, not liked him – love did not come into it. But now, in one startled second, I beheld he had become a fragile old man. His grey head was a balding desert, his shoulders stooped. Surely he had shrunk. In fourteen years, as I had altered from infant to woman, so he had been changed from a strident scholar to an aged gnome. I also reached a sudden inescapable conclusion, which was that he, like myself, must have spent the afternoon asleep in a chair.

Astonishing myself, I felt sorry for him, his downfall; more so when he called so querulously over the bannister into the lower regions of the house. But he was still my enemy. Might one grieve for a foe?

More importantly, what had he called out? My mind caught up with me, and I heard his cry again. It had been,

"Plooty! Are they not home yet?"

He would mean Caris and Thalvia. Impossible. To be safe here, anyone must be indoors by dusk at the latest, just as all livestock were secured, and doors bolted and barred. Only such creatures as chained frere pigs might be left abroad for purposes of temptation. Or guard animals able to kill.

Almost before I knew what I did I had run down the interval of stairs.

When I reached the second landing, my Uncle stared at me – aghast as if never, in all his life, had he seen me before.

Nevertheless, *They are not here!* he hissed.

"I heard you, Uncle."

Turning from me inevitably, as from something of no consequence, he strode off down the remaining flight to the lower floor. The upper air smelled of his electric fright.

I ran on after him.

Often one may act on instinct. Or it may be in

obedience to an even more feral motive. It seemed to me there was not a thought in my head, only a sort of angry buzzing, like bees.

A single lamp burned in the lower passage, and, seen through the doors, the hall had been fully lit, and the big fireplace kept bright. Euthon ignored this or seemed to. He thrust at once on and down into the kitchens, a visit he never normally attempted.

Plooty stood in the midst of the room, her hair mostly undone. She looked deranged, but I had seen that before over, to me, quite trivial matters – a lost handkerchief, a broken egg...

The moment Uncle Euthon appeared to her, and she to him, both of them began shouting at once.

Cob, who perched to one side of the kitchen table, gawped at each of them in turn. As nearly always, my presence was forgotten.

"The Mistress..."

"Caris..."

"We expected – thought..."

"Where? Why was I not...?"

From the fractured cacophony I began to piece out the arguments. Apparently, the carriage had not returned, as always it would have done well before sunfall. Plooty though had not 'liked' to disturb 'Master'. 'Master' now threatened her with the town whipping-post.

More significantly, someone must go out to search.

Only Blutch, however, would have been willing to do such a thing after nightfall, or capable of coping with the enterprise.

A deadly quiet fell, as all of us considered the dismal and hopeless predicament.

There was but one window in the front kitchen. It was partly below ground-level and looked up through a narrow slot across the grounds to the house wall, but some of the higher slopes and the hills were also visible beyond.

Abruptly, then, I noticed a weird reddish glow appearing in the glass.

I watched it a little while. I was not certain if I should mention it, or if anyone would pay attention if I did.

My dilemma was resolved by Cob, who announced, "Bit of a fire up there, I reckon."

"Fire. What *fire*?" Uncle Euthon lurched to the window.

Plooty screamed.

Until that evening I had not heard anyone really scream since I was six years old.

I felt a type of contempt for Plooty's scream, therefore. It did not compare with the shrieks cemented in my past.

But Euthon and Cob were galvanised.

"The carriage...!" howled my Uncle. "Something has attacked – it's afire – we must – where's Blutch... oh Blutch – where is he...?"

"But he's with *them*, Master..." snivelled Cob, who had assumed a crouching position.

My Uncle pounded past me, nearly knocking me down – how had I ever seen him as old and fragile?

Plooty tore after him.

Cob did not; he seemed ambitious of crawling under the kitchen table.

I followed the active participants out into the passage and so up into the hall.

Euthon plunged on through the lamplit room, past the boiling domestic fire, and threw wide the so-far unlocked doors. Outside spread the long lawn with its single spindly calcium pine. Then the high wall and the gate bisected our view. Over the wall, up there on the road, I now saw the red blaze quite clearly. It was broader, more fiery than before. And it was moving – surely it was racing nearer to us...?

"My wife – my daughter...!" bellowed Euthon.

Plooty, who had fallen back, bolted suddenly past him. In her grip was one of the old riflers. She must have grabbed it in the hall.

"*I'll* see to them!" she squealed, "I'll do it, so I shall. Since none of you has the balls he was birthed with..."

And she was gone down the lawn, through the blackness, with the bonfire stars appearing, and over to the east the grim Planet just now rising like a wodge of cyanic dough.

Give me another hundred years, I doubt despite all else I shall be certain even then why I next pelted after her. But I did.

Perhaps it was my childhood, when sometimes I would follow Plooty about, less from trust or partiality, than fear at being left alone. This was maybe at the back of it anyway. For to be left with Cob and my Uncle now must represent *total* aloneness.

Plooty ran fleetly, even in her house-slippers, bounding over the tufts of grass and next the gravel by the gate. That must have been unlocked for the return of my Aunt and, flinging it wide, Plooty flew though, not bothering to push it back behind her, just as I did not.

Sensing or hearing me she did not look round but goaded me with a breathless angry "Come on, then, you." Did she know it was only I – did she hope Cob had come with her?

I stumbled once or twice, and nearly fell as we got onto the uneven cart track that led up towards the road. Naturally I had never come out here after sunset in all my years at the house. The awful Plain, with its troughs and slopes and shallow upper ridges, still faintly glowed a dirty pale against the dark of night. Soon stars might start to fall… I thought then I heard a distant smash over towards Pitch Hill, or the hill of burial mounds, but there was no flash, so perhaps I was wrong.

In any case, the blare of fire was in front. It was definitely closer now, violently red. Not anything to run towards, I thought, as I ran.

Something quick, about the size of an ordinary rat, darted over the shale by our feet. Plooty, amazing me even at such a moment, sprang upwards, leaping right over it. She must have scared it too, for with the briefest flicker of lit-match eyes, it shot itself away into some hole.

I was unarmed. I was a very great fool.

What was wrong with me?

Unconditioned too, save by walking, (mostly through rooms and up and down stairs), and occasional harsh housework, my legs already ached and I was panting absurdly.

But I was now as scared to run back miles it seemed, when I glanced over my shoulder – as to continue.

The Plain, the night, the world, were so huge and all unfriendly. And seen from here, how tiny the ugly house was. As a shelter it was patently useless anyway. That it had ever kept anything out had been simple blind luck.

Rocks heaped the edges of the road. Plooty was scrambling over them, breathing like a rusty engine but still game.

When I stumbled after her, my legs now shaking

like jellies, I had no breath at all. Forget stars, the whole sky seemed falling on me.

I bent nearly double, croaking for air. When I straightened up, I found Plooty had also stopped, and not moved on.

She had attention only for what was coming. She gaped at it in horror. *"See – look..."*

Whether it was my Aunt's carriage or not, it seemed to come hurtling at us from a sort of breach in the dark that it had burnt out for itself.

It *was* a vehicle but wreathed in and combered by flames. Flames surrounded it, and also apparently poured from its insides, and in addition we could hear terrible shrieking, (which even so did not, in my transverse judgement, measure up to the outcry heard in infancy. Conceivably this was self-deceiving, but at least it steadied me a little).

I began to be able to make out the shape of the two donkeys – but neither had a head that I could see, even though they were running, thundering on, their armour thick with fire. Something lay draped over both their backs. I did not identify it.

By this time, the whole assemblage seemed a few feet from us. Yet it must have been at least twenty yards away.

And even as it flung closer, yet it never reached us, and might never do so.

At that very second, something thudded, in passing, painfully into the back of me. Unable to help myself I toppled to my knees. Astonishment and terror eclipsed each other, and I knelt there insanely on the road, and watched the frere pig, broken free of its shackle yet again, come to a bristling snorting standstill at Plooty's side. Its head was level with her hip. Both of them were in silhouette against the fire.

She, to my further bemusement, put out her hand and struck the pig lightly on the head. The pig grunted and shook its pins of iron fur. Unbelievably, had it come to defend her? Together they stood to meet the onslaught of the burning carriage, and only then Plooty slowly raised her rifler.

Who knew if it would work? None of the guns in the house had been cleaned, re-loaded or fired in a year or more. Only Blutch went out to shoot things, and that with his own piece.

I thought, *she will activate the trigger, the gun will blow up and kill us all, maybe even the frere. Or else the carriage will explode and do the business.*

I found, although cowardly afraid, I was miserably glad in a sodden, unforgiveable way.

Just then all the firelight went out.

It was so unlooked for, even I took notice.

It seemed a vast bank of grey fog had surged up

from the stones of the Plain Road, and formed now another wall, this without any gate.

Far above, the sky was to be seen; around us everywhere else, the Plain itself, was visible. The road too was there in the distance on either side.

But the fog-bank, having formed, was now solid and motionless as stone. Through or from it came no sound, no hint of fire. The fog had eaten the fire, eaten the carriage and the donkeys and anything else that had been with them.

Plooty gave a hoarse sigh.

She lowered the gun.

The frere pig sneezed and sat down on the ground.

Some minutes passed, most likely six hundred seconds.

My knees had begun to hurt on the stones, so I got to my feet. Ridiculously I glanced around.

Below, the house still showed its few unhelpful lights.

I believed I could make out a largish animal creeping along the perimeter of the wall there, but it might only be some actual illusion. The fog was nothing like that, of course. The fog was made of stone.

Plooty began to recite a forbidden charm. "One bead, Save Me, two beads, Rescue Comes, three beads, Trust in the Spirit..."

One did not mention the Spirit often. The Spirit, which was powerful and omniscient, had abandoned the world years ago, mortally – or etherically – offended at mankind. Therefore, to mention the Spirit in public might be a whipping offence for a woman of Plooty's station. Among the Prince's Guard, apparently, it meant a man would hang.

But there started to be a type of shifting in the fog. Something, after all, must be going to emerge from it.

There was no use backing away or screaming, so neither Plooty nor I did anything like that. I thought at the time anyway I could no longer, myself, scream.

The frere pig sneezed once more. Its hackles were well up, and one fore trotter poised to paw at the road.

Then two demonic metal faces pushed out of the greyness.

Neither Plooty nor I reacted either to this. Even though we knew them well: they were the heads of the donkeys in their armoured headpieces, and next the rest of them followed. The animals were whole, nothing missing. They were decidedly not decapitated. Nor, even if tarnished, were they on fire. After them came rumbling the carriage, tarnished also, and with much of its bodywork either black or fallen off, or hanging by a nail and dragging screeking along the stones.

The wheels made a noise too, and smoky steam coiled and uncoiled over everything, dense and reeking.

And so I saw that this was what the fog itself had been, for now it was disbanding, folding off in all directions in long, oily, stinking cascades. I could hear too my Cousiness weeping and coughing, and my Aunt Caris calling pitifully, "Oh! Oh! I thought we were for the Marble Garden – that was what I thought - Oh! Oh!"

And only then, such was my bemusement, and doubtless Plooty's too, did we notice that another figure was leading the nearer of the donkeys, in fact the very animal over whose metalled back Blutch now lay, black and cooked as a burnt sausage and, from the look of it, his spine snapped as well, quite dead.

The pig mumbled.

Plooty raised the rifler again.

"Who is it?" she screeched. "Who is it you are?"

The figure was ragged and bowed over, his back deformed, so it looked. His hair clouded him, grey like the oily dirty fog. How very disturbing, that unknown, alien filthy old face, and the large black eyes that glared, together smiling and hating from it, like two dragon-things fleering from a cave.

"Call me Olon," he answered, in a voice to sing down the moon.

2

The Garden of Lies

What I remember is that the woods were full of green treacle. This is what it seemed to be, to me. It trickled down the bare stems, glinting in the sunlight, with a weird, slow, snakelike motion. Underfoot the treacle lay in pools; it was sticky. We picked our way with difficulty, and they urged us to hurry. Some of the younger ones were picked up and carried. But I was six and thought old enough to walk. We had to reach the river. It was a long journey.

That, and my memory of the screaming, were for years my only recollection of what had divided my past from my present, and so from my future.

Blutch's body lay in the hall on the long side-sofa, which had been covered with an old sheet.

Pieces of his clothing, and it seemed of his burnt body too, had flaked off on the sheet. It was so dreadful a thing, we had laid him there, Cob, Plooty and I, in a sort of dazed shock that made us both exquisitely careful and respectful – and utterly indifferent.

"Poor soul," Plooty said at intervals in a toneless

manner. Much as now and then she also said, "And we've lost that pig."

Cob was white as china.

In the parlour, where the fire had been lit much earlier for their return, my Aunt Caris and Cousiness Thalvia sat moaning, and sometimes my Aunt would start her shrieking again. And then I could hear Uncle Euthon begging, then shouting at her to stop, he could not bear it, and Thalvia saying, "Mother, please, Mother – leave off now – we're home now – it's over…"

And the clink of the nog bottle, and then another space only of moaning and mutters.

We had, that was Plooty and I, come the rest of the distance down the slope in the company of the grey, cripple-backed stranger, who led the donkey-carriage.

All the time Caris had made a noise in the carriage, and once she had seemed to mean to rush out of it. At that the old man let go the rein, in fact handing it temporarily to me, and went back to the door and spoke to her through the broken window, now in a voice so soft I could not decipher a single word. But after this Caris fell silent, and stayed so as we resumed our path, until we reached the gate.

I, and Plooty too perhaps, had been afraid on the track to move far away from the vehicle. Only when we were almost at the house did Plooty break from us and dash straight through the gate, calling to Euthon and Cob.

When we were all inside the wall, my Aunt erupted from the carriage, and all her full hysteria broke loose. Euthon and Thalvia somehow hauled her on into the house. (Neither woman appeared physically harmed). Cob stood like a dead creature himself, transfixed by the sight of Blutch.

I heard my Aunt screeching, "They were *things* – *things* attacked us – horrible *things…!*"

I turned my head and looked swiftly at the old man with black dragon eyes. To my concern they were looking directly at me.

"Things, she says," he murmured. His voice was very beautiful, dark in tone and musically phrased. It made one listen more to how he spoke than to what he spoke of.

After a moment he added, "I'll see to these donkeys. I'm used to animals."

And he detached them from the carriage and – simply in passing – slid Blutch's body, without undue force, off the nearer animal's back, so it fell face down on the ground.

I suppose I stared. I am unsure if I did.

But then he said, "Don't bother with that. It's too late for him. But get that slow-thought there to do up your gate."

And somehow, although I barely took in his words, I found myself stepping immediately over to Cob and pushing him towards the gate. Together we locked and barred it – and it was only then I recalled the frere pig, which at some point of our descent must have run off, for it had vanished.

There was nothing at all out on the track, the road or the Plain that I could see. The burned and defaced carriage bulked within the wall, still smoking, and Blutch lay on the earth until Plooty came back. Then she and I and Cob gathered him up.

They are terrible times, where you have no idea what to do next, not even how you are meant to think or feel.

Blutch had been a brutal man, cold and graceless, but very efficient at dealing out death to beasts and birds, and in his past when a Guard, to men as well. Whatever was it that had been able to destroy him so thoroughly? *Things!* my Aunt had cried. There were always rumours of murderers, nightmare, part-sentient apparitions, such as beastmen, or bobs. Whether actual or not, they were possibilities, like all malign elements now. My Cousin Wild had been trying to frighten me that very day with such a rumour, had he not? And later I had felt the prickling unease out in the grounds, *inside* the wall -

Plooty and Cob and I were still standing over

Blutch on the side-sofa when the hall doors, which had been shut, rattled loudly.

Cob gave a yell and I jumped in my skin.

But then I knew who it was and did not need Plooty to bustle past with a snappish, "There, Girlum, don't you start off too. I'll have enough to do with the Mistresses and their goings-on. It'll only be the old man, and a good thing we've got him here with Blutch gone."

When she let him in, the hump-backed man, who had named himself Olon, stalked straight along the hall to the fire as if he owned the place. Here he stood warming himself, tangled and rent as he was. He looked a scavenger of the worst sort, the kind that previously Blutch himself would have seen off with a gun. But now the fellow turned his head as if slyly, looking out through his thick ruin of hair, and said, "Hasn't he called for me yet?"

"Who's that?" asked Plooty, crisply.

"Your prince here."

"Master Euthon," said Plooty.

"Ah, Master Euthon, then. Hasn't he called?"

Plooty opened her mouth, I imagined to tell the stranger, Olon, that he had done no more than his decent duty in saving the carriage, and he would be blessed if my Uncle allowed him to remain the night in the barn. But before she could say this or anything, my Uncle himself came out of the parlour.

He enunciated in a breaking woeful tone, "You are the gentleman then, Olon, is it? Come in, will you? We have a good fire, and drink. Come in here and speak to my wife."

The wind came that night. When it did this, it was like another living – punching at the house and its barricades. Tiles would fly off the roofs, drainpipes shift. But I had heard Plooty say the dead ride the live wind, coming by to look at their own shed corpses and to lament, chiding any who survived.

If Blutch rode the wind, there was no knowing and no unknowing either.

We sat down to supper late, at almost 5 pm, and it was after 6 midnight before anyone stood up from it.

Plooty had been told to bring in the fresh bread and cold meats from the larder, and the cake, which had been meant to stand for another week and then to last through the week after. The jars of pickled fruits were brought also, and applenog in the best bottles, and a keg of pine-beer. Our stocks would be low. Normally, my Aunt purchased foodstuffs at Flast, but on this occasion nothing was in evidence. Either the provisions had been stolen during the assault, burned or forgotten.

No one by then had explained anything of the events to Plooty or Cob, and naturally nothing to me. (Nothing really ever had been explained to me about that house, or the family, I now thought. I had learnt in childhood to survive by default, slapped or lectured when I did something wrong, fitting myself – inadvertently at first – to the acceptable scenario).

In the end I went quietly into the parlour to listen. But I had only been there minutes when my Uncle sent his commands for supper, and all of us trooped to the dining room. At the meal, my Uncle and Aunt sat as they did at breakfast, one either end of the table. But the old man, Olon, now sat down at the table too, on Euthon's right – as a rule Wild's place, when he was there.

My Uncle had invited Olon to do this.

Thalvia's place was therefore next, after the chair kept for Mhayr, to Olon. And mine across on the other long side, facing them.

The dining table however was much weightier than the one for breakfast; it was carved all over its edges and legs with animals and birds, and in the centre rose the three open carved shelves, where the food, cutlery and glass might be laid. Once these were loaded up, it was awkward for anyone at each end to see right down or up the table. While for those at the sides it was impossible to see across to the other side. And so I found it. However, Blutch was no longer able to steward. Plooty and Cob, having already borne in the portrait of dead Cousiness Mhayr, acted as servers, and I must join them. So I too carried Plooty's well-cut meats to everyone, or reached pickle for them, or slices of cake. And in that way, at various junctures, I got to witness all of it. And him. Olon.

Here, as in the parlour, he was serene and peculiarly lucid. By which I mean he seemed always to reply to any question in an assured and courteous way. Yet his words were often oblique, conceivably nonsensical – although even there I was not quite sure. As I have detailed his voice, at least to me, was mesmeric. Frankly uncanny. And I had trouble almost always in being certain as to exactly what he *had* said, so irresistibly taken was I with the pure music of his speech. Again and again, I was playing over to myself what he had said in order to grasp it. And that way I would miss half of some other utterance. I wondered if I alone was subject to this bizarre aphasia. Hard to tell. By then my Uncle, Aunt and Cousiness had had a quantity to drink, and it looked as if he had too.

But had he, for example, just replied to my Uncle's "Surely, you've previously served in some guard or army?" with the words: "Each of us is enlisted in that."

He had been speedily changed as well, that is in dress en route to the dining-room. My Uncle must have gifted him with the suit of clothes and shirt, all of which appeared a flawless fit – they had been Euthon's own some ten years before. Olon's matted hair, though unwashed, trimmed or combed, had been tied back neatly by a black cord. The oddest thing. I had not reasoned it out until then – he had no odour. Or rather no unpleasant one. From the state of him, even now, (his face and hands were still grimy, and smitched from the fire), one would assume he must stink. But his personal smell, which only now did I detect, when bending to give him food of refill his tall glass, was pleasing. It was like that of the clean fur of a healthy animal. Nor did he have any whiff of fire, which all the rest of us did.

All told, Olon was an enigma.

But he had won my Uncle over quite. While my Aunt, now calmed and a little tipsy, gazed at Olon with the bright, tearful eyes of thankfulness. And Thalvia? Thalvia flirted with him, almost outrageously, in a manner that, if she had done it before, (she had not that I had ever seen), Euthon would have reprimanded her instantly. Because it was not that flirtatiousness young women sometimes offer the useful old man – such as I had seen her use, when some veteran town officer called at the house. Thalvia flirted with Olon as if she liked him only too well, and they were besides alone behind a screen. She even began to touch the back of his hand with her fingers, and once she brushed an imaginary crumb from his slim, bitter mouth. (Oh, it was a bitter mouth, too, no lie there. But well-shaped, and not cracked dry as, in the old, mouths often are).

A strange evening.

I had eaten little, not wanted it nor had much chance. When eventually my Uncle got up and suggested he and Olon go to the conservatory for a pipe, Aunt Caris and Thalvia also hopped up, burnished with nog, and wandered out. Then Plooty fell on the cake and pickles, and Cob with her, both of them like starving whyvits.

They had no worry that I saw. The broached beer keg also stood there, and Plooty had drawn them off a couple of large stoups. They drank Blutch's dead health and Cob began to cry, and Plooty said, "Hold up. Don't waste tears on the dead, it's the live ones need it, poor souls."

After a while they also went away, and only I and the forgotten dead canvas Mhayr sat there, blindly facing each other through the three ledges loaded with meat skeletons and glasses.

I doubt if I knew what I did. Had I ever properly known anything at all? I pulled open one of the drawers of my sidetable and took Wild's oldest pack of cards. I started to lay them out in a solitary game of Perseverance.

The house beyond the door was thick with its own noisy silence. Outside the wind wowled and hit at all points of entry, shouting for Blutch or for all of us. High on the wall the biggest of the house's crescent clocks told me it was nearly half past midnight.

The oblongs of the cards were somehow cruel, and in the lamplight, now low and guttering, the faces of devils seemed to peer from their yellow, red and black designs.

Then he was there.

He was sitting there, across from me, in the Mhayr chair.

I had not heard him come in, nor had I heard or noticed him move the heavy picture. But he had done, for it leaned farther up the table. He must have moved things along or off the table shelves too, for I could see him clearly and unimpeded in the opening, only framed by all those carved beasts of wood.

"And here she sits," he said.

I did not answer. What could I say?

But I was afraid of him, truly afraid in that instant, as maybe I had not been even of the burning carriage.

"It's a windy night," he said.

As if to answer, where I would not, a tile whistled past the window and landed with a crunch outside. For a moment all the house seemed to rattle. On such nights stars seldom fell. High up the wind broomed them away long before they could drop far enough to leave the sky. And yet it was as if some very enormous star now poised directly over my head, balanced on the tip of the night's black knife, preparing to descend and crush me.

"They've taken themselves to their beds," he informed me. "They were suddenly tired. It's been a tiring day for them."

My mouth opened a little. That was all.

He gave me a sort of terrible smile. All that bitterness, and hate, and smile, all mingled and at one. He did not grant you any of it without all the rest, or else he could not. If he struck you a blow it would have a certain sweet tenderness, so if he smiled, there was the blow in it too.

"Yes?" he prompted me, my parted lips.

"How was it," I said, "you put out the fire? How did you chase away the – *things* – whatever they were – that attacked the carriage? How…?" I faltered, sorted my thought. "How was the carriage full of flames and none of them hurt – only Blutch with his back broken, and burned every inch of him?"

He sat in the chair and let his head fall back across the chair's arched top. I stared at the column of his old neck, raddled and incised with age and filth.

His wonder of a voice said this: "I did not put out any fire, for there was no fire. I did not chase away any things, nor did any things attack the carriage. They were unhurt because, stupid and human as they are, they thought in their hearts they must survive. But the man with the gun – Blutch – he believed his hour was on him, and so it was."

I rose to my feet. The cards scattered.

He said, "Come here."

But I sped around the table and fled for the door –
only this did not happen. Instead I fled around the
table and directly to him. I stopped only when I
reached the chair, and the cuff of the old-new suit
touched lightly on my wrist.

"And you were playing cards," he said. He moved
his head and gazed at me with his black eyes. His
voice was so beautiful, and so were the eyes, I now
noted well, even if they were dragons too. "Shall I let
you see, you gambler," he said, soft as a whisper, "*my*
hand?"

And then he pushed up the shirt-sleeve, and the
cuff of the coat, and held out the back of his left hand
close to my face – so close since I had, without
realizing what I did, leant forward.

The hand was dirty as all of him, gnarled, the
knuckles enlarged and split, and the nails coarse,
thickened, sallow, and some almost torn right off.
There was a dusting of grey-white hairs too, on the
hand's back, and on the skinny arm, which had a
corded ugly muscle in it. It was, in its way, quite a
repulsive hand, and a nasty arm.

And then it changed, the hand, if not the arm to
which it was attached.

The hand grew smooth and hard and strong, with
long lean fingers and short clean nails. They and it

were all scrupulously clean, as if scrubbed not long ago with good soap. The colour of the hand was palely tawny, the skin belonged to one who, though healthy and rich, might work now and then if he chose to, in the gardens or fields of Summerfall. The light powder of hair was black. The nails had perfect white half-moons, like the full crescent of a clockface. It was a royal hand, bold and intelligent, and ready to caress.

I started back as if released from a chain and I knocked the portrait of dead Mhayr, which went clattering to the floor. If I had damaged it, I neither knew nor cared.

He said, "Shall I tell you a story? One short line of it? There was a man, but his name wasn't Olon. A fine house, this. Very fine. Don't you think?"

But by then I *was* running away, had reached the door, and in the passage outside, finding all the lamps Plooty had lit when my Aunt returned were out again. I ran on in blackness and up the black stairs, up and up, never missing my footing, to my room in the attics under the roof.

Mhayr had died the year before I was brought to the house. Hers was the last funeral they had had to deal with, but they had taken her to Flast. Here, the inner town being well protected, the Marble Garden was vast, and most burials were seen to at night, with black carriages and burning torches, much singing and drinking and an all-night watch around the grave. (The do for Euthon's father too had been quite grand, even though it had taken place near the house, on the local hill and during the day, since night in the countryside was always precarious. But Euthon and Caris had had far more servants then).

Blutch's send-off we must manage for ourselves; he was only the steward besides. Yet if it had been Cob, no doubt they would only have shovelled him in the ground. (And I? I could not help the thought, what would they have done for me? I had a curious cold idea they would simply have moved me back to my attic room and locked me in there until I was hygienic bone).

There was a great fuss anyway.

Plooty and Cob had apparently kept a watch for Blutch in the hall. From certain remarks of Plooty's I gathered Cob had dropped off to sleep several times and she had had to 'stir him up'. They had drunk the keg of beer, however, and Euthon was not pleased.

But Plooty stood up to him, fawning yet adamant. "And it would be bad luck on the house surely, if no one had done it, and you and mistress, after the ordeal, were not in a fit state to honour the dead."

Soon after this, Plooty found me in the conservatory, where I had gone mostly to hide.

"The Master says you must do the Lament."

I stared at her.

"Oh, put away that face of yours," she said briskly. "It's nothing at all. Didn't I do it for Mhayr when I was only ten?"

A lie. She had been fourteen.

"You fill your lungs and let it go like a song. But your Uncle says the two Mistresses aren't to venture out, even in the afternoon, so upset still, poor souls. And I must stay here too to keep my eye on their wants."

I thought my Uncle was willing to risk me but not Plooty. After all, with Blutch gone, who else but Plooty could carve the meat properly, or fire a rifler if she had to?

She added for my benefit, "Cob will be there, well-armed. And you'll have the old man now, to help mount guard."

For a moment I looked at her, not knowing who she meant. But of course, I knew very well. Why else was I in the conservatory, at the back of the lacquered plants?

I said, "But he won't."

"Of course he will. He'll want to stay with the house so he will. And he's a strong one, that old fellow, and able. I'd bet," she added, really to herself. "He was a fine sight in his early days, when he was a young man."

I thought, *I've seen him then, as a young man.*

At least, I thought, *I have seen his left hand young.*

But I went back in the house and found my Uncle. I had seldom, even as a child, asked him or my Aunt to let me off any task, quickly judging it either useless, or all the pleading it required too tiresome. This however was another matter.

"I wish not to do the Wailing, Uncle."

"What? What did you say?" He never employed even an invented name for me. If ever he had coined one, he had swiftly forgotten it. What did I need with a name save *niece?*

"I'm afraid," I said, "I'm not able to offer the Lament."

"Someone must do it. Surely you don't expect a woman of your Aunt's standing, or my daughter, to perform it – for a steward?"

"No, Uncle. But why not Plooty?"

"You seem unaware of the awful events of yesterday. Plooty must stay in, to see to the women."

He stood in the passage with me, before the closed door of his study. Whenever anyone sought him there, and during much of any day that was where he would be, out he would sidle, pulling the screen of his sanctum shut behind him. No one must glimpse what lay within. I recalled my notion of the previous evening, that he too merely fell asleep in a chair. And also I recollected how frail he had seemed. I must not tax him. I must give in, as always.

"Suppose," I said, "my voice isn't vital enough?"

"Nonsense. A young woman, well nourished by every luxury in my house, for twenty years..."

Like Plooty, he lied. I had only subsisted on his charity for fourteen.

"This is little enough to ask of you in return, and for such a good servant as my poor Blutch."

Abruptly, my Uncle's eyes filled with tears. I was astounded. He too apparently. We turned from each other uneasily and instantly, and he said, "Be ready and in your proper dress by 5 am."

Then he slid back into the study and shut the door after him.

All the way through the house and up the stairs I had been afraid I should meet with the stranger, the old man possessed of supernatural powers. (At no time had I not believed what I had seen. What I had been *shown*). Not finding any trace of him, I reckoned he was in the kitchens, or out with Cob in the grounds, even perhaps searching for the frere pig outside the wall. Now though I heard his unmistakable voice, there inside my Uncle's study.

I froze as if a sudden frost were on me.

I strained to hear – not the voice's dark music but its *words*.

And I heard him say, "You will see I am right, Euthon."

Then it came to me that to my Uncle, and maybe even to my Aunt, Olon was of their kind, their type and class, despite his appearance. How had he convinced them of this? By illusory or hypnotic magic, demonstrably. And by the same means for conversely, Plooty and Cob took him for a staunch fellow house attendant. Thalvia meanwhile, as I had seen, reacted to him almost as a likely suitor.

When I reached my room once more and was brushing my 'proper' dress – the one for burials and other festivities – I considered that Wild had yet to get home. No one had expressed anxiety about this, as Euthon's son would arrive well before sunset – or else remain a second night with the neighbours. But now I wondered what he, arrogant, young, and so far the sole shining star of the household, would make of Olon. And perhaps what Olon would try, to subdue *him*.

For the others, plainly, he had them in his net. Only I, though he had terrorised me, he did not have at all. But evidently, *I*, as ever, would not count.

By fifteen minutes past 5 o'clock, just the four of us were trailing over the Plain, with Blutch the speechless fifth. He was borne along on the bier, a kind of open sled drawn by one of the donkeys. This donkey naturally was armoured, the metal having been scoured of smoke all morning by Cob. (If the fire had not existed – Olon's words – why and how did the stench of it linger? And then too, if even the smell were an illusion – was it his work?)

Olon climbed the slopes with us, though his tread was light, a catlike, wolflike tread. Like Cob he had been armoured-up, but Cob bore the second rifler and the spade; Olon had been awarded Blutch's long-knife and piece. My Uncle and I were not armoured. We were mourners.

It would be left to our attendants to protect us. The bier was made of wood, and quite old, ornately carved as any table, but its imagery was skulls. Blutch's calcified remains lay under a red velvet pall, and had been scattered with Curse Flowers, the dried blooms of Sealsafe and Best Memory.

Euthon wore his funeral suit of deep black, and a cravat of light green.

It took, encumbered by the sled-bier, about thirty further minutes to reach the walled hill of grave mounds.

A morbid and haphazard venue greeted us. Every family of any worth, for some hundred miles about, took their dead there and stuffed them into the hill. By now it resembled a man-made heap, a sort of junkyard or rubbish-tip, with the jagged mounds snouting up everywhere, so one could not avoid walking over some, despite its being unlucky, not to mention ankle-turning, to do so. Every grave nevertheless had its little stopper of marble, most discoloured now, for many were almost twenty years old. The marble even, now and then, had been cut with a name or date. Otherwise all types of trophies were stuck about in the earth. There were fresh and rusty knives, cups of verdigris copper, bullets, plant bulbs, (which mostly either perished or mutated to weeds or thorns), hobsteel sticks with ribbons tied on, which had been scarlet or silver or blue, but which weather had bleached and torn. Additionally, the wall was breached here and there, and creatures had come through to maraud. It was therefore not unusual to stumble on a small bit of corpse discarded as inedible.

What a tragic spot, too sad to feel anything for. One dared not, one did not. Or, if one did, it had to be soon over, like a sneeze or single spasm of vomiting.

Euthon showed no emotion. He had already presumably curbed it.

We guided the donkey along the narrow paths among the mounds until we found some patches of spare soil to choose from. There was little room. In another pair of years, surely, this Marble Garden must find an extension. Pitch Hill loomed behind, black among the chalk. Undoubtedly it was to be the next site.

It was Cob who cried for Blutch. *Poor soul*, as Plooty

would have said.

I partly believed the sorcerous Olon would go over and mesmerically quieten him, but no. And Cob anyway dug with a will, and maybe more vigorously from crying. He gouged earth from the hill, and cast it carelessly back, so grit flew in the eyes of my Uncle and myself. Did Cob wish to make us cry after all?

Olon meanwhile patrolled the hill, moving round and slowly round, never mis-stepping on the baroque surface, looking out in every direction. I too looked constantly about. But nothing was creeping. Close to midday is generally the safest time. On the road no traffic moved either. Wild had not yet come home.

Of Olon I was uncomfortably over-aware. Even when he was farthest off along the hill-top, a smaller figure about the size of my own left hand, every inch of me tingled as if doused in mild acid. Constantly, although I tried not to, I discovered myself attempting to trace some clue to his other (illusory) self. From his hands, his *left* hand, I must rip my eyes away. But that hand, like the other, was today intransigently ancient, withered brown, and sable with dirt. In my Uncle's old good suit, he was additionally horrible, like a tattered black whyvit with gilding on its feathers.

When the grave was deep enough, Cob lifted Blutch off the bier, and the pall fell back and reminded us of the state the dead was in. Cob carried him to the hole and then dropped him straight in. One heard the cluttered noise as charred flesh and bone met the earthen floor. One of my Uncle's class would have been lowered on a plank. And I was vaguely disgusted, as until then I had only seen the buryings of important neighbours on decent planks. Yet what did decency mean? Blutch was this and gone

Euthon spoke the afterword.

He extolled Blutch's virtues as a steward, his prowess in the prince's Guard, numbered his years with the family (twenty-two or twenty-six, I have forgotten). The peace of nothingness was on him and Euthon said that now his rest was well earned. His name would always be praised in our house.

Then we all threw in more of the dried flowers as Cob started to fill up the grave. The time had come for me to teeter to its edge, and shriek and wail the Lament for the Departed.

I had been dreading this very much.

Regardless I took my place. I glanced down and saw the remnant of Blutch already obscured by earth and shale and petals.

My mouth had no moisture, my throat was wooden as the bier, I could not produce a sound, let alone a Lament. For this transgression they would punish me, a severe slap, the kind suitable for an offending adult – deprivation of all food perhaps, or an incarceration in my room…

But something else drew my eye. In a sort of trance of disbelieving, I altered my focus and noted the frere pig had turned up without warning on the hill. It was trotting forward, pausing only once at some unidentified grave, to lift its hind leg and water the ground with hot, quicksilver piss. In the mouth of the pig was a slender shoot from some bush or bramble of the Plain.

Skittish yet unusually couth, it then trotted to Blutch's plot. Cob, arrested in his toil, dropped the spade and stood glaring at the pig, making disco-ordinated attempts to flap it away. But the pig paid him no attention. Leaning forward it let go the little sprig into the grave.

The inappropriate madness of this was thrilling.

Even Euthon gave a low cry.

Cob let out an awful moan, a shattering belch of pain and resentment.

I had not meant to. My eyes flew up like winged insects, and I found I looked directly at the sorcerer, right into his gaze.

He was laughing. *He* had done this. He had done all of it. *His* was the dominion, earth and air and fire – and *spirit* – that too? World without end...

The scream broke from my throat like water from a cistern. It did not hurt, though later I would feel it like a burn inside my neck.

It seemed to me I was tall as a pine, or one of the violet-purpie or taller. My head reached the sky. I had no limbs. I was a serpent raised on its tail. Shrieks and wailings sang from my voice-box, and though frightful, they were melodic and in their way had a soprano loveliness, which I could hear. They were extremely powerful too. Bronze bells might have envied me. I had no fear, no self-consciousness, no doubt, no compunction. I was not doing this for anyone. It was simply what I might do.

And as the symphony of the Lament stormed from me, I recognised in it all the screams and howlings I had heard when I was six, as never since had I heard them. And I was delighted and heartened, reassured by this. For in reproducing them and their disparate metallic agony, I reinstated for the very first time my credit with myself. I could never have done this thing had I not heard it once before. My genius was in the reproduction, but I had been well taught.

Miles below I saw them, barely relevant, the men at the grave and the corpse and the pig, all respectfully waiting on at my art. But not him. I did not see him. Olon. How could I? *He* stood at my back and held me fast, *laughing* as I sang.

Of course, though, he did not hold me. He was across on the other slope of the hill, maintaining his servile patrol for our safety. And yet too, I had felt him pressed against my spine, warm and hard as sunlit rock, and his hands had been on my waist. His voice had laughed soft at my left ear. Even his hair had brushed my left cheek. It was clean and coarsely silken, and in colour very dark…

I have no recall of how I ended the Lament, or what next I did. I do not recall, for example, moving off from the others. I do not recall going down the hill.

I *found* myself again, as if bumping into me, another stranger, only when I was below on the Plain, and walking alone with fast long steps back towards the house, unguarded by anyone.

And finding myself like this, I was obviously alarmed and stopped. Looking over my shoulder, I beheld them all in the distance, *he* himself included. Still on the hilltop. None of them it seemed, had bothered with me. They would be engaged in finishing the mound, selecting a marble stopper from the bin and hammering it home. They would chip the stone and not trouble with a date or name.

All about, fortunately, the Plain had stayed empty.

I decided the house was now my best chance, and I had better run to reach it.

But then I saw a billow of chalk dust rushing along the Plain Road from the opposite direction to that of Flast Town.

I stood immobile, stupidly wondering if one more

burning vehicle would burst from the chalk-cloud. Then, as it drew nearer, I made out the tawny shape of Cousin Wild in his gambling coat, riding his donkey as if in a race.

As he swerved off onto the track, he never noticed me, nor any activity on the hill. He looked sullenly bad-tempered. Doubtless he had lost all his cash again, and the fat sisters had either denied or disappointed.

"What? Who is it? Why let the fellow in – he might be up to any caper. Mother you're crazed. And *you*, Plooty, I thought you had a drop of brain in your head. As for you Thalvi – I've always known you were a silly cat. By my blood, I'm not out of the place ten minutes but sanity falls apart. What was Father thinking? And where…" added Wild in mid-tirade, (he was yet slightly drunk), "is that devil Blutch?"

"Oh, Wild" said my Aunt in horror.

Thalvia spat furiously, "You were told not a moment since. He was *killed* when the – when the *things* attacked – our carriage!"

"Things? What things? What were they? Man? Animals? Oh, beastmen maybe?" he added with utmost sarcasm, forgetting also possibly how he had tried to frighten me with the rumour of just such a being. "You were asleep and dreaming. Why, the carriage isn't even scorched. I saw it in the carriage shed as I rode in"

"It is. It is!" shouted Thalvia "And how dare you speak to our mother and myself in such…"

"I'll speak how I like to a house full of silly bitches"

At this, everyone, even Wild himself, fell quiet, such was the impact of his impertinence.

And the door of the hall was opened and in walked my Uncle, limping slightly from the long funeral trek, Cob behind him clutching the spade, and not a hint of any other man.

Immediately, Wild straightened himself up and paled down, trying to cover his behaviour as an animal might a turd.

"Father Is Blutch dead?"

"Dead. Dead and buried in the earth, may his rest be complete"

"Fuck the Spirit," breathed Wild.

They all chose to overlook his oath; at least it was not blasphemous since the Spirit had been insulted not invoked.

My Uncle turned to Cob. "Get out, you fool, and put the spade away."

Cob went docilely and the hall doors were shut.

Euthon glanced at me. "I saw Plooty slip out. Fetch her back."

She had indeed slipped away as soon as Wild turned his attention from her. So I went to the kitchens, and getting there of course found Cob again, now sitting at the table with his long face nearly dropped into the wood of it, while Plooty poured him applenog from their secret store.

"My Uncle..."

"Wants me. Well, he can wait a little. I have been up and down that stair forty times if I have been up once. I have enough to do."

"Well said, my girl," said the voice, from the hearthside.

I had not even seen him there. Or he had not allowed me to see him until that instant.

Plooty tossed her head and at once one of the ropes of her black hair got loose and fell down her neck and breast. At that normally she took umbrage. Not now. Now she laughed. But patting Cob on the head she left the kitchen with a tray of blue-tea and jams for the hall. "Let them be waited on by a bird-scare, then."

Cob drank. The other sat in shadow at the fireside.

The other spoke:

"With Blutch gone to earth," said Olon, "Cob is the only man fit to be steward."

That was not true at all. Cob would be useless at the task, as he was at so much else. Cob did not answer.

In the half dark over there, the old man did not look old. His hair looked as dark as when it had, (in my imagination only?), stroked my cheek on the hill. Every so often one of his black eyes flashed off a sequin of light from the flames.

He said, all music, "Are you not, Cob, fit to be a steward? Surely you are. At the least. Or even to be the Master here, maybe. Do you never dream of being a Master? Or the young one, perhaps, the tipsy brown one who shouts in the hall?"

From this I gathered Olon had glimpsed Wild, although I was uncertain how he had, unless he had spied him crossing the grounds, or even through the keyhole of the hall door.

There were stamping footfalls outside in the passage. It was not Plooty coming back, that was definite.

The door crashed open and there stood Wild, seemingly summoned by Olon's reference to him.

"Oh, so *that's* it is it?" he bellowed. He had a bad voice, Wild at the best of times, vile when he was enraged, as now. His anger which had tapered off upstairs was towering again. The whites of his eyes were pink as a frere pig's, and he had a high colour too, as if fire burned there inside his head. Or was it only red liquor from the neighbours' house-still?

"Oh, so *there* you *sit*, you scavenging quorel of a *thief* – drinking our tea and eating our food and no doubt your *snout* in the *bottles* too."

(In fact, there was neither liquid nor any food in front of Olon).

"Well, you may have pulled the blanket over my

Father's head, but you won't do it to *me*. Stand up, you waste of mortal breath, and get yourself off outside these walls. It'll be dark soon enough. Best hurry."

At this Olon rose.

Coming up beyond the glow of the hearth, I saw him as I had formerly, dirty and old and grey. But he looked straight across at Wild, and Olon's mouth curved in the most – how to say this – *seductive* smile.

"Oh, so *that's* it?" repetitiously ranted Wild, clenching his fists. "Want to gamble on me, do you? Well, I can put you out, you old leech. Do you think I can't?"

Olon moved in a manner I did not follow properly. He seemed to pass right through the table, but must have, I reasoned, moved around it. He was abruptly there before Wild.

Olon was rather the taller, even in his stooping.

Wild leapt back and pulled back his right fist too, then slamming it forward at once, to plant a violent blow on the old man's mouth.

But instead Olon's hand was somehow interposed. It caught Wild's fist, and all the force of the blow was absorbed as if by a great invisible pillow. And then Olon stood there, holding Wild's fist firmly, nearly *kindly* in his eldritch hand. And leaning down he kissed Wild gently and graciously on the lips, as a mother might with a child.

In this way I saw it, what was possible to him, to Olon.

Cob did too, for he had cranked his head up to watch.

Wild's face went, not pale but bloodless, and he sank slowly down on his knees.

He knelt before Olon, and then, with a fearful lunge, he grabbed and buried his face in the cloth of Uncle Euthon's cast-off good trousers. "Ah – ah – no, – ah…" he choked. Did he weep?

Olon stayed a moment by him, letting this curious rite go on. Then he simply moved away and back to his seat at the fire.

At that Wild curled up on the floor and sobbed and dribbled, and then fell asleep suddenly. He snored.

Just as I had before, I myself backed away. I went out of the door and ran upstairs, past the living rooms where I could hear their now quite ordinary-sounding voices – Euthon and Caris, Thalvia and Plooty. I went into the library, and there on the table lay one of the books, open, and a piece of a page staring up in the fading light of afternoon.

I thought – *What is he?*

I thought – *I can never know.*

I thought – *I imagined all this too.*

I thought – *He is a demon and has put this page here for me to read, for after all he will communicate with me as well, since no one must be left uninvolved in his scheme, whatever scheme it is that a demon hatches.*

Night spread in the sky like a blot of ink.

In the house, the lamps had been lit this evening at the proper hour, even the three in the passage outside, for I had heard Plooty go up and down, her skirt whisking along and she humming some tune under her breath. I could smell the oil from the one leaky lamp too; I always could when first it was lighted.

I sat, not at the table, (I had not looked again at the opened book), but in the high-backed chair by the middle window. Once a single but huge star fell, miles over towards the town. It was like a silver ribbon on fire, but too far away to project the noise of its crash.

As I sat, sometimes I thought about the Lament I had given and how it had matched and honoured the screams I heard when I was six.

I could remember so little about that day fourteen years before. No one had ever asked me to speak of it, indeed Caris had said to me several times that I should never say *anything* about such business. I should rather try to wipe the events from my mind. When I replied that I had slight memory of 'the events', she said I was fortunate and must be grateful.

Sometimes in dreams... the red place, or the other place which was yellow, with the sun a kind of blur, and then purpleness like a long shawl trailed over the light... and the sounds, not only the shrieks, but a low rumbling, a sort of growl, or it might have been thunder.

After that, a void divided the past, until I was in the woods of green treacle. There we walked for days, nights. When we reached the river it was full of lumpy shapes, which may have been corpses, but actually I believe them to have been fallen trees, slabs of disturbed ground from the banks, stones – and on one occasion, which I recollect mostly because the boats had difficulty in manoeuvring past it, an enormous shut wardrobe, some eighteen feet wide.

While I sat at the window after the star fell, my eyes abruptly went blind. That is, an opaque glowing oval filled their centres. This had happened now and then for some nine years. It never lasted long, but was horrible and fearful, for I was used to be able to see, and like this I dared not move. I sat therefore with a jittery enforced patience, trying to count off the seconds on my fingers. But I soon grew confused. The blindness could distort my mental perception too. Once or twice, in the grip of it, I had talked gibberish, stammering. I remember Caris slapping me. Perhaps her cruelty helped, for that time the miasma cleared from my vision instantly. I had been grateful, but I was then only eleven years old.

I could dimly peripherally discern the edges of anything I looked at, around the opacity – the window, the curtains, the general unlit dark of the room. My ears were not influenced, and so I heard when the door opened.

Did I really mean to? I said, "I can't see. Not for a moment."

Another would have cursed me for an idiot and said I should light a lamp, for the people I had lived among had no grasp of such things as my evanescent blindnesses.

But he was no other.

He said to me, softly, clear as light in my ears: "Look at me. You will see *me*."

And I knew *he* did know I was blind, and that also him I should see. So I looked.

But oh…

Oh, what I saw, for see Olon I did, was a man nearly seven feet in height, whose head was only a foot below the lintel of the library doorway. He shone, right through the stigma that had disturbed my vision, like pure young marble. But his hair was blue-black fire and his eyes were black silver, as the falling star had been across the night. What he wore I could not determine; it was simple, pale. Behind him something stirred like two compartments of a storm. That I could *not* make out. Yet there was a scent in the room I was conscious I would never have detected if I had not in those moments been otherwise impaired in physical sight. It was the aroma of outer limits, galvanic, cold as ice – upper skies – and the black nothingness beyond.

And then everything swirled away and resolved, and I could see regularly once again. And the old man stooped there in my Uncle's cast-off, with one of the lamps, (the leaky one), in his left hand. Had I only picked up the flavour of the oil? Now there was nothing else abnormal.

He crossed to the table, glanced down, said, "So you've not read that yet. I left it for you to read."

"I know that you did." After those spells of blindness often I was not quite my more cautious everyday self.

He said, "You've lived all this while, what is it – fourteen, fifteen years? - in this graveyard, this Marble Garden of a life. Naturally, you can't yet break free of the stone that encloses you. But if you won't read, I'll tell you a story."

He sat at the table and pushed the book along a little, placing the lamp where it had lain instead.

My vision now was very acute, as if to deny its lapse.

The lamp beamed yellow on his face. He looked a hundred.

"Now the Spirit," said Olon, "lived in a wonderful country, like a magnificent, extraordinary garden, and at that time, all humans lived there with it. This was in antique days, of course, before the Spirit abandoned us to hell-on- earth and humanity began to hate the Spirit.

One morning, and in those times a morning could last all one glorious sparkling year, some people – and they don't say who – went to the Spirit and said, *We have a plan, something we'd like to make.*

And the Spirit who, then, was always kind and reasonable, answered, *What plan is this?*

But when they had told the Spirit, the Spirit seemed unhappy and alarmed – not for itself, that was, but for them. And the Spirit said, *Go walk in the garden for a while. Let me consider this."*

Olon paused.

I felt I was expected to offer a remark.

Perhaps he judged I must comment on his benign, therefore blasphemous, use of the Spirit's name. But that seemed irrelevant to me, and maybe it always had.

I said, "The Spirit was the parent, and we the children."

"Exactly. But a wonderfully wise and magnanimous parent. And wonderfully beautiful and intelligent children. The Spirit, then, was so proud of them it would break your heart to have seen it. Never mind that. Two of the people went into the garden. Perhaps they were the two that had most directly asked. He said to her, *I told you not to ask it. It will say No.* But she said, *I must go and look at that tree. It needs some pruning.*

So, he sat down and began to talk to the grass which, there, could converse, while she went into the orchard.

The tree she had in mind was a big, tall apple tree, and the fruit that grew on it was made of emerald. Do you know what an emerald is? If not, a green gem, translucent when polished, transparent when cut. These apples however were all polished and gave off a smooth luminescence. She, the woman, reached up and picked one, and stood there turning it in her hands. And when she had turned the emerald six times, from behind the tree there came a gigantic ratine. He was a handsome fellow, big as a man, and his hair combed down all over like silk. And she said to the ratine, *I asked, but the Spirit will say No.*

The ratine said, *Ask again. Haven't I explained already? All this is pretty enough, but how much better you can do it. Think of the design. Do you see that apple in your hand? Why not create a country in the same shape, rounded that will spin in space? You will be the rulers there. You can do as you want. Or do you want to stay a child forever?"*

The lamp on the table fluttered. For a second it went green, like the apple in the story.

Olon said, "The rest is easy to relay. She left the ratine and took the emerald to her male human companion, and said to him, *I can make these better.* And he, dazzled by the emerald, or by her, agreed.

And so they went back to the Spirit and begged and pleaded, and nagged and sighed, and sulked and wept, and boasted and vaunted – and gave it no peace.

So, in the end the Spirit said, *If truly you must, then I must let you."*

Olon raised his eyes. My acute ones, newly washed by their failure, saw metal in his pupils now, and in the irises of his eyes more metal, and rushing rivers and star-clotted nights. And the nothingness, that also.

"The thing they made, then," he said, "which they knew they could make better than the Spirit could, was another garden, another world. But where the Spirit, which was perfect, could make nothing that was not equally flawless, what these humans made in their enthusiasm and arrogant haste, was a work of genius – but a genius corrupt and also that of a great fool. They therefore created a mess of a world, and so that is ours. The Spirit's country had been called the Garden of All Truth and Beauty. But now I'll tell you, shall I; the name of *this* love-forsaken shit-heap?"

I looked at him.

Then he had risen and was by the door.

He said, "Its name is the Garden of Lies. And…" he amended very gently, "here, emeralds don't grow on the fucking trees."

The Gardener

3

The Gardener

I began to think mostly of him. I was already largely only *aware* of him. I spied on him, followed him in whatever way I could, sometimes merely by looking from window after window of the house.

But frequently too I would go down to the kitchens and so find him there with the house-people. At the three main meal-times, the breakfast, the tea, the dinner, (or at lunch if ever lunch was to be eaten by the family together). I sat on my central isolated chair, and watched, *watched* his every move, but dissembling where I could, as best I could, and avoiding his direct gaze.

He sat on the family side. His chair stood between those of Thalvia and Wild, while dead Cousiness Mhayr had been moved along beside Aunt Caris's place. Sometimes he even carried Mhayr, her portrait, into the room and propped it in its seat. He was as strong or stronger than Blutch and needed no help with the cumbersome thing.

Examining him so intently, he seemed always changeable, to me. Now straighter, now more stooped and crouched; just fifty years old, next a hundred and fifty. Only his hair appeared sometimes dark, and young, or his face – in shadow or against the fierce light of a fire or the sun.

Now *he* paid me no attention. He was like the others in that. But it was *not* like that at all.

It seemed to me his utter inattention was a game we played, he and I, our secret joke that no one else had found out.

I tried hard and always to resist this sense I had of that.

But I did not sufficiently succeed.

At night I would lie awake an hour or more, and he would crowd out all other notions and concerns – but then, what notions or concerns had I really had all those years?

I did not dream of him then. Not once. Unless... but I shall come to that.

I decided I should have liked to dream of him but prevented it. Which perhaps is not only an insane idea, but presumably unlikely.

I had not however read the page he left for me in the opened book in the library. I did not have the confidence to risk it. The book lay there and was not moved. Even Plooty, when (rarely) she dusted the table, would leave the volume and page exactly as they were. She herself, beyond a smattering, could not read words.

Yet had its placement meant something to her?

Now and then at night, when I did not sleep, I did consider going down to look at it. I never obeyed the impulse. And otherwise, by now, I was seldom in the library.

He was my dilemma, my enterprise, my pastime, my obsession – my religion too. For religion was dead in the world, officially at least. There were those who still invented some form of it, clandestinely, a perversion in some hidden room of the mind. Olon became for me that other alternative. He was both refuge and entertainment – these are the wrong words, but they encompass what I mean. I dreaded him and longed to see him. I was terrified he might go away as abruptly as he had arrived among us. I titled myself mad, but *they* were too, surely. How could we not be, now? I felt more comfortable since I was entirely lost. But I was not, entirely. Not yet.

About two days after the incident with the burning carriage, one day after I had given the Lament, Olon began to go up to Thalvia's room about 1 am.

Naively, although I had heard her door open below long after she retired, I did not think it was he. Sometimes Caris had gone in there, very late, to reprimand or talk to her. Caris had for years, as I did now, slept badly. And certainly I thought, once I realised that not she, but Olon, entered the bedroom in the earliest hour of morning – often not leaving until another full hour had gone (I timed his visits). I supposed Caris too must hear what went on.

I have to say it was not any loud footfall that alerted me, only the creak of the door. Each of the doors of the house did creak, and each rather differently from the others. One did not consider this until such things happened, and the doors became traitors.

Initially there was no other evidence. Then, three nights later I heard Thalvia cry out several times in a frenzied frightening way. Still, given those previous screams I have so often mentioned, almost instantly I grasped Thalvia's were not of the same order. Quickly I worked it out. I was no innocent, only ignorant, and for that matter a virgin. Snatches of chat in the town, or from Wild, even Plooty, had informed me inadvertently of the noises men and women might make in the tumult of sexual spasms.

Six nights after I first heard Thalvia's noise so clearly, I heard the creak also of another door – Wild's. And not ten minutes after, there rose the most appalling racket. It sounded as if furniture – the bed? – was leaping and springing around on the floor, while my Cousin himself made a sort of nasal mooing that reminded me only of the bovinids I had seen in pens at Flast. And when this ceased, after some five more minutes, Thalvia's door creaked again, and next she screamed so long and loudly I could not think my

Aunt and Uncle had not heard her, even if deaf to their son's former transports.

All this dismayed me. Once again, I find no better word. Yet too I was fascinated. And I ached with an aroused lust which, then, I could formulate no label for, and made explicable to myself only as envy and rage.

I would pace about my attic and remember he was old and foul, that I did not and could not 'fancy' him, as the well-served Wild might have said.

But I *did* fancy Olon, evidently, fancied him with the desperate desire of one starving. I knew, after all, even if my outer mind did not, he was not in any sort what he mostly seemed.

As for Plooty I was so convinced she had lain down or, for that, stood up with Olon, I did not waste thought on it. She had been available to Blutch, even to Cob now and then, for several years. Only Wild did she put off, for he was not of her 'kind'. And she had always been too fly to let him snare and abuse her. But Olon, or his semblance, was to her of her 'kind'. Just as to Thalvia, demonstrably, he was of hers. As to Wild himself, who previously never ever, so far as I knew, or anyone did, had a liking for buggery.

Time passed. The nights were busy. I think indeed every night was, but I was beginning to sleep again, worn out by my vigils, and my obsession.

By day none of them gave any indication of their

antics with him. And he himself neither. He checked the grounds with Cob or sat in the front kitchen with him and Plooty, or in the higher rooms with the family. Thalvia and Wild now treated him with respect, but also with a sort of detachment – as if he were an elderly relative, some grave scholar who had always dwelled in the house.

It was when it seemed to me my mood had quite settled, albeit into a sullen feral discontent, that I dreamed the only dream I recollect from that stage in our proceedings. And at first I did think it a dream. But later I knew it was no dream at all. It must have happened. Then again, I did *not* believe this, and it was relegated to the status of dream once more. Or even to a vivid, half-waking fantasy. To this moment, yes even now, I do not know which it was. I have never confronted it, let alone any other with it. In a way, I see I have come to reckon I made it up, that it did not happen in any fashion, not asleep, nor awake. For it seems to me it is a symbol of all and everything. Something which cannot be yet was. That was, and is, real – yet is not real, as perhaps nothing is real ever.

I had fallen asleep and I woke. I thought another star had woken me, hitting the roof or the grounds outside. It was cold and I had seen them every night inflamed and red, all ready to hurl themselves off the sky. But nothing had come down for a week or more.

I meant to turn, then found I could not. I lay on my back and something lay over me. It was warm and heavy, and covered all my body from my shoulders to my feet – only my face and throat were free of it. I was not for a second fearful. It had a smothering quality. I could not move, yet it was wonderful to have this smother and covering on me. One wished it to smother. Wished to be enveloped and imprisoned and held flat to the mattress, and never move again.

The room was totally dark – that is, I could see nothing. I had never known it so before – there was no light anywhere. However, this too was not unpleasant. It was not like any sort of blindness. Although, robbed like this of vision, one might concentrate on sensation.

But I put up my hands to find what had covered me over.

I felt at once the large, firm and youthful body of a man, long-limbed, and with a long and muscled back, smooth as planed and burnished wood, yet tactile as velvet. Below the back the lean rounded buttocks that must accompany such a back, and the thighs, also smooth and muscular. The thighs were lightly sheathed in a slight grass of hair that, even in the blackness, made itself known to me as also black. Becoming aware of this, I became aware next, or simultaneously, of the front of him which lay on me

89

so profoundly. The hair on his breast was finer, but further down at his centre, thick and harsh, it seemed to me like the black wool of a hill sheep. His mane fell over us, the black hair of his head, like a thick curtain of silk, far softer tonight than I had felt it on me in the graveyard. And I felt the scentless breath of his mouth and nostrils on my face, calm breath and cool, regular as a silent tide. His own face was raised up above me, his back fluidly arching like that of a snake. I knew he looked at me and saw me as if in clear sunlight, though to me he was invisible. I knew he was Olon. But it was the other Olon I had been shown, the left hand, the visitant I saw when I could see nothing else. He had the scent of fur and leaves, and of a kind of barely discernible spice, which sometimes grew a little more evident, then sank away. Suddenly, not reasoning what I did or why, I threw my hands upward into the air above his arching back – as if to discover some continuation of him beyond his skin. I felt a curious whirlpool in the dark a moment, like a breeze that stirs along the earth at the end of Summerfall. Nothing else. And then I forgot this, because he had lowered his mouth and his hands to my breasts.

No human man could have managed this. He did not support himself as any human must, on his arms. His arms were free. No, like the snake I had been reminded of, only the power of his lower spine held him those inches above me, effortless, and let his lips and tongue, palms and fingers, the deluge of his hair, ripple their caresses over and over without interval.

I had never toyed with myself, resisted it doubtless, if ever tempted by any feeling or instinct in youth. That was a strict household. They would have been made plain all the evils I must avoid; through little hinting lectures I could not even recall.

The shock of his touches then was initially almost hurtful. I thought I did not like what he did, then that I could not bear it. But soon it changed. I wished it never to end.

He did not once kiss me. He only tended and worked on me and watched as I became molten and a mindless thing, that moaned and shivered beneath him. Lightnings and quakes seemed to be approaching through my body. I could foresee no destination that could conclude this paroxysmal trance, or else I thought it physically impossible. Finally, some other element of him began to rub at me, there where my sex was. It was not his male member which did this. I never felt his prick, nor had that time any indication of it. Instead, this other thing, a sinuous, flexible almost creature, like some attached yet separate animal, slid and tickled, then grew insistent, demanding though never quite invasive, pushing itself ceaselessly over and along and against the core of my body – until my womb melted like crystal in me, and huge surges, like drumbeats or bells, rang through that closed inner tunnel; kicks and punches of ecstasy, repeating to infinity…

But finite, for the delight sank at last like fire died at its term, like bereavement.

And there I lay, cast up on the shore of night, with rivers and seas singing in my ears; and no one was with me. I was alone, and I was asleep again; I had been asleep all the time.

In the morning, I examined myself. I was unaltered. Nothing had happened. I felt even so I should not like to see him ever again, Olon. Yet I went down, and he was old and repulsive, and he had not been with me, and I could not be abashed and afraid, because I had dreamed it, obviously. After a time, it nearly amused me. It was my private joke. *He* was excluded. Nothing to do with him. Only mine.

We had had a spate of fine bright days, colder than ever, the sky white as good teeth and the sunlight sharp as broken glass.

One morning before midday, Wild, who had ridden off at sunrise, came back with one of the fat neighbour sons. I had seen *him* only twice before, a charmless specimen. He stood by the chicken sheds, drinking nog with Wild.

Presently Cob came along and let the chickens out,

all of them, there on the grounds. The cream and brown splashes of their forms, droppings and feathers were scattered far and wide. Bevies of them flew up into the violet trees. A few others took their clawed way into the fruit-garden. Some had red crests and crowed like rusty bagpipes. No one seemed to think any of this a silly mistake – even when Plooty's ratcat came slinking around the side of the barn and sprinted among them.

That was when Olon appeared anyway. He scooped up the ratcat and hung it about his neck, where it leered from its grey eye.

"This is our new man, Olon," said Wild to the fat neighbour.

Wild spoke now as if very proud of Olon, but because he owned him, or was related to him, I could not tell.

"Oh, Olon then," said the fat man, dismissing whoever and whatever Olon might be. To Wild the fat man said, "I'll take them off your hands. They're fit enough. They'll settle it."

"Good, good," said Wild. "Mark you, I'll have them back next month."

"Surely. Why not," said the fat man. "Drop by when you've a mind. You know Muna is always glad to set eyes on you."

"Oh, Muna," said Wild. "I thought she had another suitor."

And they both laughed, and then Wild and Cob,

and the fat man's own man, began to gather the chickens in a collection of cages of wood and wicker, and a couple of very big and ornate ones perhaps once used to house parrots or tame whyvits. These were next loaded on the neighbour's donkey-cart.

I was staring but Plooty had come out too, and I said to her, "Why is he taking my Uncle's chickens?"

"Oh, to cover Wild's gambling debt."

I was astonished. Wild always lost, but Euthon, when he had to – often – covered the losses himself in cash.

Soon almost every chicken, even those dragged from the fruit-garden with tomatoes in their beaks, had been caged and loaded. Only two refused to descend from the grove, climb up and shake the boughs as Cob and the fat man's man did.

"Will you take tea?" Plooty asked subserviently.

"No," said the fat man, and to Wild, "I'll get back."

And off went the cart at once, rattling, crowing and clucking.

"I'll fetch the last eggs then," said Plooty, resigned, uninterested. "We won't get any more, this side of Summerfall."

I wondered if my Uncle and Aunt knew of this predation on the livestock, and that soon there could be no more cakes.

Who after all would risk going to the town? But

perhaps they would, if *he* went with them. Or had they begun to tell themselves anyhow they had dreamed it all? I had seen the carriage by then. It was tarnished, but not really as if it had run through fire and spouting fire from its every orifice, as I had witnessed it. Or thought I had.

Cob had not repaired the loose plates and armourings, but they had been shabby a great while. Only Blutch's dead absence seemed by now to prove, at all vehemently, that anything had happened. But no one mentioned Blutch anymore.

At tea that afternoon, when the lamps were lit and the fire high on the parlour hearth, and we sat at the smallest table in our usual positions, (I all alone), I waited for anyone to refer to the chickens. Plooty did.

"Enjoy your cake, Master Euthon. There'll be only enough eggs for two more." This time she did not even give a date for feasible renewal.

But my Uncle indifferently nodded, and my Aunt Caris indifferently said, "Tell Cob to come up and see to the fire."

There was also the frere pig.

Looking so often from windows to see if Olon were outside, and when he was what he did there, I eventually spotted the pig.

By day, normally towards sunset, it roamed along

the Plain beyond our walls. It seemed preoccupied, and was sometimes accompanied, during the four sightings I had of it, by a ratine.

Despite the mating habits of these beasts, I had never seen told that they escorted each other in this manner. But then maybe they would not frequently have the chance. Now the pig was permanently loose and did as it wished, the ratine was available as its faithful companion.

During my fourth viewing, which was at night when I could not sleep at all, the ratine danced for the pig, writhing and rolling and skipping about. In the moonlight it brought the pig gifts too. I could not be certain what they were, for both animals were far up the slope towards the road. Probably the presents were squeamish items, prey the ratine had killed, for example.

Did they cohabit now on the hill of burial mounds? It seemed they might, for the pig alone, or both together, they would always trot away in that direction.

Endlessly, the graves on the hill were molested. One could only do so much for the dead. But for the pig and the ratine, such a domicile would be ripe with bonuses.

The two chickens roosted in the trees. One even laid an egg there which dropped to the earth and was smashed.

Plooty's cat ate it, yolk and shell.

But less than another twelve days had passed before the chickens flew away, and the ratcat went off as well and did not return.

Stars fell constantly during the following nights. Even so, none fell on the roof.

In that way, now, I was woken solely by intrusive silences, or the ghostly orgiastic cries of Thalvia or Wild, which seemed to grow, if not less violent, then oddly less loud. (Had I screamed in my dream – in my real undream? No. I had sobbed. I did not like it that I had wept. But I was glad that, whatever the cause, no one was likely to have heard me. Or if they did, would not guess the reason for my sounds).

Besides, I sensed the hearing capacity of my Uncle's house was failing. It and all of us were going deaf to certain things.

And I thought, *Shall I too go away? But where?*

I had never ever thought this. Even in childhood when they ill-treated me, I had not.

But I did not go away. Olon was in the house.

When did I first notice how changed they all were? Partly I must have been primed to it for weeks, but not coherently. The metamorphosis crept up on all of them, as on the house itself.

Now and then at the edges of Flast, inside the town's outer wall but excluded from the inner ring, one saw an abandoned house. Even I had seen such houses, on the rare excursions I had made there with my Aunt. Something had occurred in these houses, illnesses, deaths, some sort of integral structural malaise. They were deserted and shunned, and eventually pulled down, leaving gaps where the town itinerants set up little camps amid the weedtrees soon rioting there.

My Uncle's house was now coming to have a similar look to it.

I only saw this when, going into the grounds, I noted the outer gate had been left ajar. I ran to secure it. No one had gone outside. I had just passed Cob in the yard and he now was the only one of us likely to do so. Having locked and barred the gate, I turned and took in the house. It stood about four hundred yards off across the spaces of lawn and shale, gardens and sheds. Seen that way, in the persisting razor-edged sunshine, it was like the habitat of dolls, but careless ones, or maybe plague-ridden ones. The building appeared slightly tilted, out of true. The walls, (they looked like stained cardboard, such as cheap dolls' houses might have), bore strange blotches as if wet dirt had been rubbed in there. The glass cards of the windows glared blindly. As my eyes must during my visual affliction. From the chimneys issued faint smokes, like faltering breath.

While I walked back, the house, becoming bigger

again, gradually seemed more usual. So that from some hundred feet away I believed I had been wrong. But then again, bizarrely, as I went ever closer, the signals of collapse and desuetude re-emerged and were worse. Now the marks on the walls were like actual *bruises* in skin – or more likely, the discolouration that shows on a corpse as it begins to decompose.

Perplexed and alarmed, but not sorry, (I had always loathed the place), I noted the drains leaning off the sides as if pulled out by giant vandals. Vast drifts of roof tiles lay with the remnants of stars along the front. I could clearly make out the black gaps in the roof left behind. There had always been leaks from the roofs in various sections of the attics. Cob repaired them on occasion, but they always reasserted themselves. There was a leak in one corner of my room that had been there years. Recently I had not found any water collected in the bowl I left beneath it. Perhaps, I thought, now about to gain the full run of the house, all the other leaks had persuaded mine to go elsewhere with them, where there was more to be accessed and ruined.

I paused to glance in at the fruit-garden. Brambles had sprouted and were climbing the trees where, those few weeks ago, the briefly liberated chickens had flapped and pecked. The fruit of the lemon vine had turned a venomous puce. Bricks were out of the garden wall also.

It occurred to me that I had glimpsed cracks, even little holes, in the outer wall.

When I came to the conservatory door; that was open. I had not left it so. I went in and saw many of the painted leaves had fallen or been torn off the mummified plants.

I went to the kitchens.

Cob was there, and in a parody of throwing down a pair of killed chickens or rabbits for dinner. He was in the act of tossing a small live snake in front of Plooty. "By the barn," he declared.

From my limited knowledge, I thought the snake was not poisonous.

"Did it get in through the outer wall?" I uneasily asked Cob. "I thought I saw a hole there..."

Cob's whole face seemed to evolve in one compact lunge from that of an unprepossessing and shoddy human male idiot to the roaring mask of some lion-creature, such as were kept in the zoo gardens at Flast.

"Oh, and so I'm to fix the wall too, am I? Who're you to tell me to go out and do it? You answer *that*."

Startled and now very cautious, I replied, "It isn't up to me."

"No, nor is it. You pin your mouth shut, then."

I said nothing. I had been instructed to be silent and

was already well used to such stern orders, even if not from Cob.

But he was not eased.

Picking up a plate from the table, at the far end of which Plooty was mixing something for a soup, Cob flung it at the hearth stone. Here, of course, it shattered.

Plooty said nothing either, to my surprise. She only nodded.

Cob. with an assertive lurch, turned back to me. "Just watch yourself," he further advised me. "I'm brimmed over with service to the likes of your sort."

And going to the bigger chair by the hearth, he collapsed into it. Taking out his pipe and turf-tobacco he began to fix himself a fat smoke.

The snake meanwhile ebbed around a jug and slid, a silk ribbon, down the table leg. How fast it went, like spilled oil, and away under the door. Some minutes after I passed it in the upper house, but it was still slipping along, this time towards and then out of a side door. I formed the oblique but immediate opinion it found neither the house, nor the grounds, to its taste. Through the narrow window by the door I watched it pour on across the shale and the lawn, and finally from sight.

In the days which followed I several times noticed a similar phenomenon. Some animal would get in through one of those unmended cracks that Cob now apparently scorned to see to, but would then decide it had no advantage in grounds or house, and soon remove itself from the vicinity.

Once a plume, even, was in the fruit-garden. I spotted its feathery tail among the briars, and prudently stepped back. But in seconds it scrabbled along the spoilt brickwork and bounded off to the fault in the outer wall it must have entered by. It was gone in moments, frisking its tail as if to shake off all trace of us.

After Cob had displayed his full temper and contempt to me, where I could I kept well clear of him. But Plooty too began to be awkward with me. In the past I had evidently made her cross or mockingly amused. She believed me slow-witted and brushed me from her path. She allowed me such privileges as to wash my hair in the back kitchen where the pump was, in a manner that was teasingly cruel: "Oh, well, shall I let the poor soul rinse her greasy locks? Well, then, let me think. Ah, why not, why not?"

As a child I had sometimes been slapped also by her, but she had not been too unkind. I had to learn my place, as with all of them, in fact. I was unimportant, useless but harmless, and might be allowed to exist. Now, however, from that juncture of

Cob's flash of rage, Plooty seemed to draw her cue. She became abrasive. That very evening she showed me her new plan with me.

"What in the name of skin and blood are you at in here?"

(I had at last re-entered the kitchens, hoping to locate Olon).

"Well, take yourself out, you shambles. Go on, be off, or I'll have the broom to you."

This was all rendered in a purple scowl of wrath. But next she came after me as I started to leave, caught my arm and hissed, her spit stinging my eyes, "You bitch fuck, do you think I like the look of your rat's face?"

All this was shocking to me in its own fashion. Yet it had been burgeoning some while, and even as I focussed upon it, I knew I had already dimly foreseen them both, the ruin of the house, and the violence on the boil in Cob and Plooty – only I had been too inured to take the lesson in.

I went up to the hall and climbed the stair onto the gallery where the mirror was.

I stood a little time looking at my shocked-white face. My eyes had grown very large. I noticed in myself no other modification.

Then my Uncle and Aunt came into the hall, and gazing down at them, I was struck again by the revelation of vast changes which I had unobservingly been seeing grow in little stages all this while.

Both now were like querulous elderly infants. They clutched hold of each other and doddered to the fire. She assisted him to sit. Then she herself slumped onto the adjacent chair. They looked pathetically old and virtually mad – not in the way of those who are modestly insane, and strong, as in the past I had beheld them.

And they chittered to each other, stretching towards the fire, and she was even pointing at it, saying to him in a grasshopper tone something about the pictures in the flames, and was *that* not like the tall market tower at Flast? And there, was *that* not like a carriage – *but it was on fire* – and at this each of them *laughed*.

He was nowhere at this time, by which I mean visibly. I had not located him. I had only heard that voice of his, music, sorcery, only that, and always somewhere else in the house, as he talked to some other. Never was he where I could find to look at or listen properly to him.

I leaned on the rail of the gallery. Everything that went on here was due to him. He was... remaking – *unmaking* – all things to do with the place. For a second, I was almost triumphant, as if I had been awarded some valuable role in the downfall of my enemies, even the dirty house itself and its enclosed prison of grounds.

Then, as if impelled I turned slowly round once more and looked into the mirror. And I saw the sign on me also, the mark of destruction. It was quite hidden. It was quite indelible.

A day came. I can no longer recollect how much time had by then elapsed since first Olon entered our lives – theirs, mine. Then, it seemed to have been several months. But the season was the same, Winterspring still. We had even had a sprinkle of snow that morning.

He was there at breakfast. Plooty served the prail in the china bowls.

She gave me nothing, which by that morning she never did. But there was bread on the table, rather unfresh, and I cut a slice and spread on it some of the rancid butter. I ate this slowly.

The clock showed nearly 4 am. The sun was up but sheathed in greenish snow-cloud.

Silver-gilded by the snow, the world looked better, if more cold.

"Hurry, Thalvi," said my Aunt with cobwebby briskness. "We can't dawdle if we're to go to town."

Thalvia gazed at her, not comprehending, nor caring.

"There are only a hundred minutes in an hour – only a hundred seconds in each minute. I can't make them longer!"

It was the worn-out and familiar truism. Thalvia today did not react. She seemed incapable of most reactions. She was sluggish, voluptuous, *sleek*, passing the spoonfuls of prail into the large warm cave of her mouth, her lips rose-red, her shadow-smudged eyes half shut. She had risen from a damply rumpled bed of love. She did not bother about this phantom trip to Flast, not even enough to *say* she did not.

Wild was drinking liquor from the neighbours' still. (He must have had it an age, from well before the fat brother turned up and took the chickens, for Wild had not been to see the neighbours since). No one remarked on Wild's bibulous consumption. Wild tipped a cup or so on the prail too and watched entranced as the oats turned thin and russet.

Cob went past the window through the yard, bearing Blutch's rifler. Cob strode upright in a mechanical ferocity as if *he* now were the member of some Prince's Guard.

Euthon turned to Olon.

"Have you ever, in the town, been to the theatre there and sat through the drama of the man who wants to ascend into the sky?"

And Olon answered soberly, "I have considered the drama."

"And what did you think of it?" Euthon's voice

was brittle as toast.

"A great deal."

"I heard," Euthon expanded, "it was a travesty."

"It would be, of course. Men can't ascend. They fall." Olon paused.

I stared at him as always now I did, when he did not turn anywhere remotely in my direction.

"Just as others, other men of a different kind – that is, unhuman – drop down to the earth."

"*Stars* fall," commented Aunt Caris. "They never used to, but they have ever since…"

Thalvia, abruptly alert, leaned across to her mother and shook my Aunt's arm suddenly and roughly. "*Hush!* You mustn't mention that ever! What are you thinking of? Have you gone *mad*?"

Flustered, Caris, an old, embarrassed baby, was close to tears. "Oh," she whispered, and "oh…"

But Olon interposed; his the one voice of beauty and substance; his the only authority. "Stars fall," he agreed. "But are they only stars, which fall?"

At that moment the portrait of dead Mahyr slid, with a startling rasp and thud, off its chair. It fell heavily, unlike, presumably, stars or falling men, and struck the floor hard as it fled, feet first, under the table.

To my slight interest, it fetched up against my own chair, on its back. I looked down at it, and into the blonde painted face of the Cousiness I had never met. Would she have been gentle? Would she have been compassionate towards me? I doubted it.

Then I moved my feet away from her with distaste, for something odd was happening with the canvas. It was bubbling as if a very hot liquid were spilled on it. Even as I watched Mhayr, body, face and blondness, was expunged by a riven and encrusted stain.

My Uncle and Aunt sat petrified. They looked like two mice frozen on a cupboard-top at the entry of a lighted lamp. Thalvia however yawned. And Wild let out a deep and almost symphonic belch that seemed to scale at least three octaves.

And it was then too that the door opened from the yard, and in marched Cob, armed Guardsman to a Prince, who saluted us, or more probably Olon, and then – angling the rifler – fired directly at the ceiling.

The awful bang and explosion shook the room. Plaster dropped in chunks, and one of the invading leakages of ancient rain began to trickle through.

"*Despot!*" yelled Cob towards my Uncle. "I'll serve you no longer. I won't. I never will. I will not serve you!"

Because so often I was ignored, even then as their final extremity approached, they forgot me still. No doubt the more feral among them – Plooty, Cob, Wild, possibly Thalvia – would have remembered me later. But I had recognised at once that the last acts of whatever went on, had now galloped right in through the door of the house and its life. Without a word I got up and quietly left the table and the room, unnoted, or *if* noted, filed only for future attention.

I always ran away. It was what I had learnt to do from the time of the sticky green wood, and ever after. Run or walk, absent myself, if cornered become small and nebulous.

I made my way upstairs, and as I did so, heard the noiseless void that had succeeded Cob's gunshot only then erupt in outcry.

I quickened my pace. I darted up and up, thinking I must seek my room in the attic. Perhaps I could turn the rusty key and lug the chest, full of mildew and the family's rotted clothing, against the door.

I considered also climbing out through a window, somehow negotiating the roof, getting down - how? - into some place where by now briars clustered.

It was early in the day. Might I, if I ran fast and carefully, reach some neighbouring farm? The fat neighbours were many miles off, but there were one or two smaller more sordid domiciles that might shelter me, at least through a night. Or they might well not.

But all these plans, if they were even worthy of the name, would be difficult to execute, and more probably hopeless: could *I* climb up and *down* a roof, find shelter among the antipathetic locals, who anyway would most likely not know who I was and drive off or shoot me on sight?

The attic too was hardly defensible. I should never be able to shift the chest that far.

Below, their cries had eased. Yet I heard the monotone of Cob's revolting voice droning and blundering on and on, apparently in an unstoppable diatribe. He might well murder them all. All, that was, apart from Olon.

No, Olon could not be threatened, or harmed. Was he even *vulnerable* to physical harm? I doubted that.

I found I had gone only to the library and stood looking in. Abruptly I moved inside and closed the door. It could be as simply undone or broken in as any of the others. This was not a refuge.

For sure not. Glancing about, I saw the big hollow space as if I had not come in there for a year. And I was shocked again, stupidly unnerved. I had *known* all the while what went on, and if I had edited out the clues and notations, still I had seen them from the corners of my *inner* eye.

For the library was decomposing too. The great broken stacks, with their volumes and fragments, sagged or had completely given, shelves and bits of book and paper lay all along the floor. Leaks of rainwater, or that morning's snow, dribbled or rippled down. Moss grew velvet green on edges. Puddles of water reflected the windows, in two of which were panes cracked in the shape of glittery spiderwebs.

I had compared my Aunt and Uncle to mice. A proper mouse sat delicately eating the spine of a book. It was plainly not afraid of me. And yet, constantly it squinted about. This was a feast, but it had deduced, instinct honed, that great danger would still come. It was ready to escape at a second's warning.

On the table, one single open book lifted the white and black face of a page. It had been doing this a while, ever since he left it there for me. The table and the book and the page had not a speck of water or lichen on them. Even dust seemed not to have settled there, although I could not suppose Plooty had cleaned the table, let alone the room, for weeks.

Now I *must* look at the page.

Now was the hour for it.

He would not protect me. Yet had he left some guide, some formula for evasion, safety? Olon might do anything. It could be typical of him, could it not, to offer a solution to the only person here who counted for nothing?

I bent to the page.

Half of it was taken up by a woodcut, hence the sharp appearance of black and white I had detected all across the room. Had the drawing always been on the page? No? Yes?

It was a bleak and disturbing image. Like the house now, it showed shatterings and crevices, yet nothing had come down. Despite their excisions, the illustrated walls still stood. And something stood also *upon* them. Black dominated the fluctuating white, with its lines of stones and spindly weeds. Distance and perspective were there too. Down and down one looked, to a rectangular and unevenly flat surface. There was a feel to the whole picture of emptiness, and menace – and of something, however reluctantly, *pre-agreed*.

The four sentences above were distinctly punctuated, even where unfinished.

I read them, and they made no sense to me at all.

No answer was here, no method of survival or compensation. A threat there was, but not specifically, I felt, aimed at me. It was a threat displayed and available to anyone. And in addition, it was obscure, if epic in its own limited manner.

I went from the book to the central window and looked out. A kind of fogginess was in the sky. This veiled far off things, such as the hills. Gauzes of icy mist clung along the Plain.

Somewhere a clock struck. I could not think where. But it was almost midday, 6 am. Had I been in the library so very long? It could not have happened; my bladder at least told me that.

From the house no human sounds rose. Only a by now steady architectural shifting and creaking and grunting, the intermittent dainty snaps and whispering rush of wooden beams and plaster, eaten away as if by armies of termites, letting go and gushing down.

I began to fantasise that the mist and fog gathering outside were being spread from the house as it rapidly gave way.

I did not know what I should do.

But when had I ever known? I had been taught I was powerless and not worth any effort, even from myself.

Suddenly, I went back and caught up the book from the table. I flung it straight through a cracked window. I was transfixed as the unprotesting pane splintered and the book flew out, free at last.

The day passed. Again, it seemed to do this more swiftly than was natural. At 1 pm. the sun was setting, although not meant to do so until two.

Olon could alter time, then. Was it only that?

Westward the sky was a powdered-over bronzen-rose, a decayed blush masked slightly with chalky mist. The rest of the sky, murky pastel ice-grey leather, hung out in the east a tooth-white full moon.

The baleful Planet was invisible. There was something dismally static to all this. And the sunset and afterglow lasted much too long. While the moon's upward rising was very slow.

In the end, when the crescent clocks reported one quarter to 4 pm, I took my way down the watery shifting house that otherwise gave no mortal sound.

Not then daring to risk Plooty and Cob's domain of the kitchens, (and now unreasonably hungry), I went back towards the breakfast room. It seemed to me there would have been no other mealtimes observed, nor had there been when I peered round the doors of the parlour and hall, in one or other of which usually tea was presented.

Of course, Plooty might have cleared the tables, but I guessed she had not, nor had she.

And in the room of breakfast, the yellow drapes on the walls were wet as baths, and on the table lay the china bowls cemented with unfinished prail, and stale bread, and the blue-tea smelling like a swamp in its pot, and rancid butter, and Wild's reddish liquor spilled and spilling from table to carpet.

The glass window-door to the yard stood wide.

Beyond waited gathering dusk in a green-grey shell, one-eyed with its darkling moon.

But my Uncle and Aunt sat in their chairs where I

had last seen them. Her head was thrown back and his drooped forward. I thought they were fast asleep, and next that Cob had shot them, and I had not heard. But they were neither asleep nor shot, merely dead. Their double wreckage of faces was peaceful and nearly self-satisfied.

See, they wordlessly said, *you can't do better than we have.*

Conceivably they were correct.

Wild was in the hall. He lay like a rug before the fire, which had been neither lit nor cleared that day.

Wild did not look smug or peaceful. He seemed angry. He was a rumpled and twisted rug, as if someone had kicked or caught their foot in it.

But he too was dead.

Thalvia stood in the parlour. She was gazing in the smaller mirror with the gilded frame carved like a rose garland. Her hands were raised to secure the jasper pins that held up her dark hair, and she still kept the sated full-lipped look she'd had at breakfast.

She made me start.

I had anticipated she too would be dead.

Then I saw she was.

Prettily upright, hands raised to tidy her hair, face fixed in self-contemplation, even so Thalvia's lissom frame was devoid of the life-spark. There she stood.

And there I stood, transformed to a silly lesser copy, live-dead in my surprise.

At last I went up to her. I touched her. Her hair remained soft and lush, the skin of her cheek was smooth, and only cool. I attempted to make her right arm move a little, but already it had changed to iron.

When I put my hands on her shoulders and tried to shake her, she did shake – just a miniscule amount. But it was like the teetering of an ornament.

I thought she would not have been abashed at the pleasant way she seemed, couth and lovely, and eloquent in her utter post-mortem petrification.

After this, I believed Plooty and Cob must be dead as well and went along to the kitchens.

But they were not, not they.

They sat at the table with the kitchen pot of tea all full of spices, so the air drizzled aromas of blue-leaf and cinnamon and nutmeg. They were carving up between them the last egged cake and shouting joyously to each other of their liberation.

And Olon sat there, about two chairs' space from them, eating the cake too and drinking the tea.

I doubted I had ever beheld him so elderly and decrepit. He had become an old, crumpled grandfather, two hundred years maybe, his eyes even pinkish and filmy like the mist over the sunfall, his still-thick hair like a tangle of grizzled wire that hung down him to his backside. He was rail-thin and hoop-hunched. His thin, claw-like fist trembled as it managed the teacup or the cake. For the very first, he stank, like a corrupted pond.

It was all now a lie, all just his acting and his game. My hatred lashed its barbed tail deep within my vertebrae, but such a response was instinctual and inept. I was his, too. He would soon be rid of me.

Yet in I went, to the table, like a thread the silver needle draws through the tough antagonism of a cloth.

And Plooty looked and saw me. And Cob saw me and began to rise up, ready to kill me at last with Blutch's rifler that leant, like his best friend, at his side.

Olon spoke. "No, let her sit. She's mine."

His voice had stayed beautiful. It filled the house.

Cob paused. *"Her?"*

"Do you grudge me that?" said Olon.

He looked upset and insulted, pathetic and whining – but his voice was notes of music full of hilarity and disdain.

Cob dropped back in his seat. "Welcome to her."

It was Plooty who bridled now. "Aren't I enough for you, you old bugger?"

Olon's eyes fixed on hers.

I wondered how she did not shrivel or burst. But she had been his lover. Perhaps that made her immune at least to some of it. (if not Thalvia or Wild). I, naturally, had not been his lover at all. I had dreamed or imagined things, that was the sum of my claims.

And too Plooty did not really know what he was, that is the sort of *creature* he was.

Her hair was all loose, and when she shook it at him, I saw or remembered she too was, in her way, pretty.

Olon said to her, "You? More than enough. But she's to be your servant."

He turned his eyes then to me. This time I met them – what point in evasion?

I cannot describe it. It was like nightfall or freezing cold, like drowning when the ice of the pool gives way and one sinks under, and the water closes like a lid.

But I felt as if another turned my head – surely he did – and I looked instead at Plooty and nodded and, fascinated, I heard myself say, "Oh, let me, Mistress, let me serve you…" in a bright, almost happy voice.

And Plooty laughed. And she picked a tiny piece of the cake from the plate and threw it me, and I caught it in both hands. I was starving. I might have eaten anything.

And Plooty said, "Well, there. Poor soul. But next time, catch the food in your mouth, you dolt. Will you like me beating you?"

"Yes, Mistress," said I, even through the cake. "It will be very fine."

I was less convincing now. I had no care for any of it, only to eat.

Not long after that, Cob leant sideways from his chair as if to pick something up from the floor. Instead he sagged right over and toppled off on to the floor himself. The friendly gun fell after him, as if it had to. They lay there then, he and the gun, unknowing, and I knew Cob too was now dead.

Plooty only smiled and reached for the teapot and poured herself another dose. I hoped she would not throw a full cup at me, insisting I try to catch it in my teeth. Plooty did not. She gazed in at the tea and began to stir it with her forefinger.

"You see things in tea," she said. "Or the tea leaves after."

"What do you see, Plooty?" he asked.

"An old wandering woman promised me once," she said, "I would have a lucky life and go to the Spirit later, but that was before the Spirit was so cursed and went away. Where will I go, then?"

He said nothing.

Plooty removed her hands from the tea and folded them in her lap and sat back in her chair. She was dignified. "To another place, I suppose," she answered herself.

"There is no other place," said Olon, in the softest way, as if to comfort her, for there were tears in her eyes.

"Then there's nothing, like they tell you on and on," said Plooty.

"Only here," he said, and then, after a space as if he had thought it out, "and there."

Plooty shut her eyes. A single tear ran from her left one. She breathed outward in a quiet sigh and never took another breath.

Some of the roof fell in, and part of a chimney, about 5 pm. By then no one living remained in the house.

"She's mine," he had said.

But I was no one's, nor my own.

I have no recollection of how long I sat at the table. The fire died too, and the kitchens grew cold, and when I rose and glanced round for the old man (the demon) he had vanished.

Then the two lamps both went out.

And through the window came a ghastly coloured light.

I sprang up and pressed myself, craning, against the glass to see.

The kitchens lay lower than the rest of the house, as I have said, and the ground there was feet above the sill. Beyond spread the sky, now glutinously black.

Not a star was to be seen. But the moon had got up high. Something had happened to it. It must have been attacked, but what could attack a moon? The round surface had gone a raw terracotta red, as if it were cut and bleeding. Down it too ran watery streams of shadow, presumably some element of the night that had dissolved.

The awfulness of this struck me mindless. But as I was staring, an eight-legged beast passed across the slope above.

At that some sanity returned, for I saw next by that same red light of a wounded moon, that the monster was the two donkeys, moving along in unison, and with the carriage already attached behind. They wore no armour. Even their heads were unencased. Another bent and bestial figure led them towards the lawn and the distant wall gate.

She's mine. In what way? If in any way, did he still mean to leave me here, alone in the collapsing tomb?

Up to the house I pelted, flying out into the porch, which shifted beneath my feet.

"Don't go! Don't leave me behind! I must come with you!"

All this echoed from my own throat, but I barely knew my own voice. I sounded like a girl again, eleven or twelve, still capable of desperation and a belief in – not rescue – but at least the chance of help.

Neither he nor the animals paid any heed. He did not look back or answer, nor did he hesitate. The carriage wheels rolled on and the hoofs of the donkeys clopped over the short moon-rusty grass.

So I ran to catch up. And as I passed by the broken bricks of the fruit-garden I heard a chimney crash and then a dull deep thud behind me, back inside the core of the house. But I did not turn to see, only ran faster, and at the gate I reached him.

"I must go with you."

"Who told you so?"

Who had?

"I am the only one you didn't kill."

"Oh, and did I kill them, then?"

"Yes! You!" I shouted very loudly now.

He and the animals and the carriage went on through the gate, blocking it off from me, and I grabbed one of the half-loose plates still adhering to the vehicle, and trotted along holding to it, and so out on to the blood-lit Plain.

"You," I repeated. "Who else?"

"Didn't I tell you; they die when they think they shall."

"No, it was you. The moon," I added. "The moon's bleeding. Is that your fault?"

"Everything is my fault," he replied. "Wouldn't you say?"

I wanted to lie down on the earth, but I gripped the

plate and the carriage seemed to go faster, and so I ran again.

I thought, *If he gets on the box and whips the donkeys, I shall never keep up.*

"Stop!" I called. "Why won't you stop?"

To my amazement the donkeys were halted. The carriage came to a standstill.

There was, I noticed instantly, a vague drumming under the ground. I had thought it only the vibration of the carriage. The whole edifice of the night seemed pulsing with the approach of some fresh and alarming event. Would the moon fall? It must be that. Stars fell. Why not the moon, then?

Perhaps I should have more sense than to speak to him again, or if I did I might pose some relevant question. But my voice threw itself out of me. It asked, "Why have you done this?"

"It is," said Olon, "what I do. But I do many things."

Worlds behind me I heard a strange whistling note and then a vivid enormous gasp. The gasp might have been human in origin but was too large. The moment it ended a sprinkle of light little explosions scattered over the upper air. None of this seemed connected with the moon.

Until then, however, all our shadows – mine, his, those of the animals and carriage – had been slanting one way, muddy and reddish. Now all the shadows were changing direction, fading where they had been, and becoming solid and very black as they pointed off from us, straight up the slope. The moon-redness rivered around them, brighter and more bright. It was scarlet now. Everything was flaming red.

I flung about and saw the ugly house engulfed in beauty. It was filled by fire, which even as I gazed, blew out of all its windows in showers of spangles, and through its several doors in curling ruby plumes like those sewn on fine hats. The conservatory detonated, firing off bullets of glass. Every dying bramble and fruit in the choked garden shone and bubbled, was uncorked to splash the night in twenty mixed fragrances of wine and jam.

The vacant chicken sheds and pig-abandoned barn cast their timbers and metals, bolts and bars, high in the air with a sort of radiant glee. Outhouses banged like punched brown paper bags. Everything was spinning itself up at the sky, as if to replace all those jettisoned stars.

Even where we stood, such a way off, small tokens buzzed high overhead. Sparkles and gold chips and jewels of embers dropped all around us. I flinched only routinely, barely conscious of being now and then scorched. The donkeys shuffled and tossed their heads.

And I turned again and saw, as the house blazed

more powerfully, the blood and burn of the moon was cooling and going out. As it paled, I noted only its old scars were on it, nothing new.

A molten silver globule whirled through the sky and landed at my feet. It singed the ground. What had it been? Perhaps a pendant of Thalvia's, or the silver handle of a dinner spoon.

But more and more silver was falling straight down. This was cold rain.

The old man began to lead the carriage up towards the track, not now moving quickly, and it was easy for me to follow.

When Blutch had forced Cob to see to the lawn and the fruit-garden, sometimes there had been a bonfire. A gardener burnt to clear old wood and prepare the ground. It was, they said, bracing for the soil.

The rain thrust by us. As I plodded on, I felt we were swimming upwards through some river.

When we reached the Plain Road, I looked back again and the fire still thundered red, unquenchable and lordly in the tumult of waters. From the sole remaining chimney, a hilted sword of crimson flame and smoke had pushed up, and stabbed the night above it, forming a scalded cloud. It did not seem to move, or ever lose its shape. Constant and unalterable, this image was then my last sight, and most abiding memento, of my Uncle's house.

Miles we went along that road, and everything was only a dim, rustling dark. The moon westered, in the rain like a melting plate. Once or twice things made ominous sounds, but a long way off. I believed I saw stikers cross the road behind us an hour after we started out. I may have been mistaken.

As the rain lessened, to me every little bush or clump of stunted trees represented savage animals. But the glitter of eyes was surely only the light of the lantern he had lit on the wet of rainy shale and flints.

Though reduced, the rain did not quite give up.

There were no dwellings I saw, although by day, I could recall, (from my rare journeys to and from the town), two or three such places had been visible from the road. But it was past midnight by then. Any human habitation would contain only the sleeping. Either that, or some other fate had seen to them.

I was blasé, I now note. I had lost nothing after all but my unloving prison. And found nothing but the seduction of the abyss.

Despite having the carriage, neither he nor I employed it. Both of us walked, as the donkeys did.

But then, just as the healed moon was quite ordinarily yellowing low in the west, the last of the rain ended. And, hit by the uninterrupted horizontal light, I became aware of what led me on.

For now, now truly, it was him.

And I moved forward, and nearer, and *slunk* up to him, not close enough to touch, only to *see*.

I had never, in my life, witnessed anything like him, nor like the state in which he was. I know anyway, or think I do, even had I been accustomed to the state, he would yet have astounded me. He would have burned me up, as the house and the moon had been. But if I was the house, which perished, or the moon – which recovered, I can never say. No, not even now. No, I cannot.

He was not seven feet in height, if for a second he looked to be. He was six feet and six inches and then six moments more, much less than another inch, moments, as I say, as if his height were also time.

His skin was young and so was his body. It was the frame of a strong and healthy man, lean as a lion, twenty-five years, maybe, or a very little more. He had the gloss on him of burnished wood, not dark nor white, the shade of clarified ale. Every part of his physique was without flaw. And his hair was black as – not night, but night's shadow. *It* rained where the rain had ended, down to the very base of his spine. And somehow also it threw a type of rain-shadow upward, behind him...

When I went on, moving around him, then walking backward before him up the road, I beheld his face, not as I had ever thought to in the past. Young, yet his face, sculpted firm on his bones, had an oldness in it that was *youthful* – in the same way as his height – like *time*. Everything of him was of such a great handsomeness and beauty it stung the eyes. It was like unfiltered alcohol. One drank and must have more and was done vast good by it – yet none at all, despite the pleasure.

He was entirely naked. Obviously, he had no requirement for garments, except for disguise, to play games. But like the pelt of an animal, he wore nakedness as a suit of clothes; their fit on him had no equal. At his loins, the black night and rain of his hair resumed, but hid nothing. As he walked, he carried his sexual organ upright as any sword.

I have said, I had never seen any man like this. But ever after, where I have, however grotesque they are, or pleasing, that first sight of him on the road after the rain, robs them of any significance. He was *not* human, yet he had gained and donned humanness. He wore it for convenience and for appetite. And because it *suited* itself to him better than to any human thing. *Him* it *loved*. This though, was he himself. This was not any shape-changing. That was for the rest.

He looked over at me only once, under his black

lashes, out of his dragon eyes. Young dragons though they now were, still they waited in caves, and still their brains were stocked with fire.

But the look: it was flirtatious, friendly. *Ah now,* said the look, *dine on me if you want. I don't deny you. You will be going to repay me.*

Still I walked backward up the road.

Still he walked forward and led the placid donkeys.

I gazed.

He stared by me at the way ahead.

The moon set.

Perhaps it would not rise again.

Perhaps it did not.

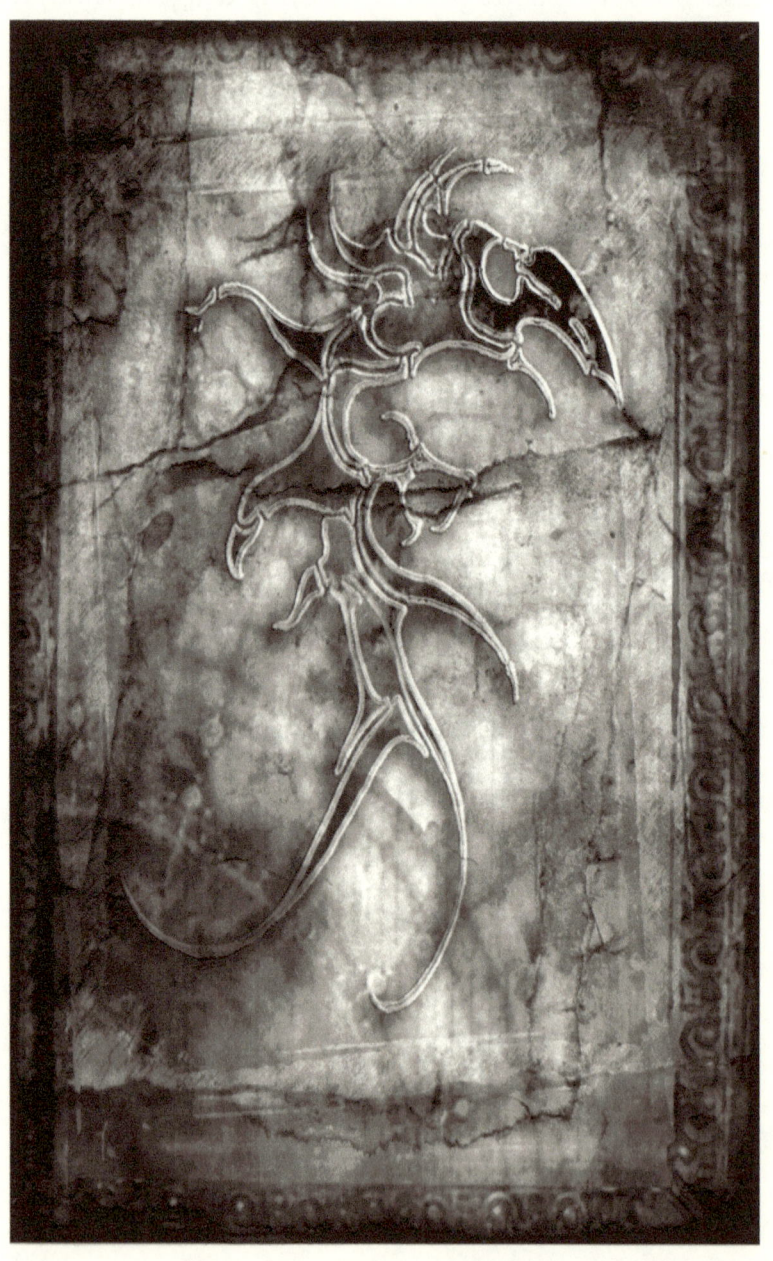

About the Author

Tanith Lee (1947-2015) was born in London. Because her parents were professional dancers (ballroom, Latin American) and had to live where the work was, she attended a number of truly terrible schools, and didn't learn to read – she was also dyslectic – until almost age 8. And then only because her father taught her. This opened the world of books to her, and by 9 she was writing. After much better education at a grammar school, she went on to work in a library. This was followed by various other jobs – shop assistant, waitress, clerk – plus a year at art college when she was 25-26. In 1974, her career as a writer was launched, when DAW Books of America, under the leadership of Donald A. Wollheim, bought and published *The Birthgrave*, and thereafter 26 of her novels and collections.

Tanith was presented with a Lifetime Achievement Award in 2013, at World Fantasycon in Brighton. During her lifetime, she also received the World Horror Convention Grand Master Award, as well as the August Derleth Award and the World Fantasy Award for short fiction (twice).

In 1992, she married the writer-artist-photographer John Kaiine, her partner since 1987. They lived on the

Sussex Weald, near the sea, in a house full of books and plants, and never without feline companions. She died at home in May 2015, after a long illness, continuing to work until a couple of weeks before her death.

Throughout her life, Tanith wrote around 100 books, and over 300 short stories. 4 of her radio plays were broadcast by the BBC; she also wrote 2 episodes (*Sarcophagus* and *Sand*) for the TV series *Blake's 7*. Her stories were read regularly on Radio 4 Extra. She was an inspiration to a generation of writers and her work was enormously influential within genre fiction – as it continues to be. She wrote in many styles, within and across many genres, including Horror, SF and Fantasy, Historical, Detective, Contemporary-Psychological, Children and Young Adult. Her preoccupation, though, was always people.

Books by Tanith Lee

Series

The Birthgrave Trilogy (The Birthgrave; Vazkor, son of Vazkor
[published as Shadowfire in the UK], Quest for the White Witch)
The Blood Opera Sequence (Dark Dance; Personal Darkness; Darkness, I)
The Flat Earth Opus (Night's Master; Death's Master; Delusion's
Master; Delirium's Mistress; Night's Sorceries)
The Lionwolf Trilogy (Cast a Bright Shadow; Here in Cold Hell;
No Flame But Mine)
The Paradys Quartet (The Book of the Damned; The Book of the Beast;
The Book of the Dead; The Book of the Mad)
The Venus Quartet (Faces Under Water; Saint Fire; A Bed of Earth;
Venus Preserved)
The Vis Trilogy (The Storm Lord; Anackire; The White Serpent)
The FOUR-Bee Series (Don't Bite the Sun; Drinking Sapphire Wine)
The S.I.L.V.E.R. Series (Silver Metal Lover; Metallic Love)

Novels and Novellas

34
The Blood of Roses
Companions on the Road
Days of Grass
Death of the Day
Electric Forest
Elephantasm
Eva Fairdeath
The Gods Are Thirsty
Kill the Dead
Heart-Beast
A Heroine of the World
Louisa the Poisoner
Lycanthia
Madame Two Swords
Mortal Suns
Reigning Cats and Dogs
Sabella
Sung in Shadow
Vivia
Volkhavaar
When the Lights Go Out

White as Snow
The Winter Players

Young Adult and Children's Fiction

Animal Castle (picture book)
The Castle of Dark
The Claidi Journals (Law of the Wolf Tower; Wolf Star Rise,
Queen of the Wolves, Wolf Wing)
The Dragon Hoard
East of Midnight
The Piratica Novels (Piratica 1; Piratica 2; Piratica 3)
Prince on a White Horse
Princess Hynchatti and Other Surprises
Shon the Taken
The Unicorn Trilogy (Black Unicorn; Gold Unicorn; Red Unicorn)
The Voyage of the Bassett: Islands in the Sky

Story Collections

Blood 20
Cold Grey Stones
Colder Greyer Stones
Cyrion
Dancing in the Fire
Disturbed by Her Song
Dreams of Dark and Light
Fatal Women
Forests of the Night
The Gorgon
Hunting the Shadows
Nightshades
Phantasya
Red as Blood – Tales from the Sisters Grimmer
Redder Than Blood
Sounds and Furies
Tamastara, or the Indian Nights
Space is Just a Starry Night
Tempting the Gods
Unsilent Night
Women as Demons

Tanith Lee Titles Published by Immanion Press

The Colouring Book Series
The Colouring Books Gallery 1: Greyglass, To Indigo, Cruel Pink
Ivoria
Killing Violets
L'Amber
Turquoiselle

The Blood Opera Sequence
Dark Dance
Personal Darkness
Darkness, I

Novels and Novellas

34
Ghosteria Volume 2: The Novel: Zircons May Be Mistaken
Madame Two Swords
Vivia
The Heart of the Moon

Collections

Animate Objects
A Different City
Ghosteria Volume 1: The Stories
Legenda Maris
The Weird Tales of Tanith Lee
Venus Burning: Realms: Collected Short Stories from 'Realms of Fantasy'
Strindberg's Ghost Sonata and Other Uncollected Tales
Love in a Time of Dragons and Other Rare Tales
A Wolf at the Door and Other Rare Tales

Of Interest to Tanith Lee Enthusiasts…

Night's Nieces

This anthology is a tribute to Tanith Lee, comprising short stories written shortly after her death by some of her writer friends to whom Tanith was a profound influence and inspiration: Storm Constantine, Cecilia Dart-Thornton, Vera Nazarian, Sarah Singleton, Kari Sperring, Sam Stone, Freda Warrington and Liz Williams. With an introduction by Tanith's husband, the artist John Kaiine. Illustrated throughout by the contributors and with photographs from Tanith Lee's personal collection.

IMMANION PRESS

Purveyors of Speculative Fiction

A Wolf at the Door by Tanith Lee

Includes 13 tales, most of which appeared only in magazines or rare anthologies. 'A wolf at the door' implies hidden threat – until the door is open, we don't really know what's out there. And now the beast is upon you, scratching at the wood, its hot breath steaming on the step. Will you survive the encounter? Perhaps, once the door is opened, what you might have thought to be a threat turns out to be something else entirely. But of course, it can also be a werewolf...
ISBN 978-1-912815-04-3, £11.99, $15.99 pbk

Breathe, My Shadow by Storm Constantine

A standalone Wraeththu Mythos novel. Seladris believes he carries a curse making him a danger to any who know him. Now a new job brings him to Ferelithia, the town known as the Pearl of Almagabra. But Ferelithia conceals a dark past, which is leaking into the present. In the strange old house, Inglefey, Seladris tries to deal with hauntings of his own and his new environment, until fate leads him to the cottage on the shore where the shaman Meladriel works his magic. Has Seladris been drawn to Ferelithia to help Meladriel repel a malevolent present or is he simply part of the evil that now threatens the town?
ISBN: 978-1-912815-06-7 £13.99, $17.99 pbk

The Lord of the Looking Glass by Fiona McGavin

The author has an extraordinary talent for taking genre tropes and turning them around into something completely new, playing deftly with topsy-turvy relationships between supernatural creatures and people of the real world. 'Post Garden Centre Blues' reveals an unusual relationship between taker and taken in a twist of the changeling myth. 'A Tale from the End of the World' takes the reader into her developing mythos of a post-apocalyptic world, which is bizarre, Gothic and steampunk all at once. Following in the tradition of exemplary short story writers like Tanith Lee and Liz Williams, Fiona has a vivid style of writing that brings intriguing new visions to fantasy, horror and science fiction. ISBN: 978-1-907737-99-2, £11.99, $17.50 pbk

www.immanion-press.com
info@immanion-press.com